**You're not going to have
a friend in the world.**

I said, "How about if I pay you and Dad rent? Then I can live here, but I won't have to be the child. I'll stay in my bedroom and come out for meals. The rest of the time I'll do what I want."

"You do that anyway," Mom said.

"It would be a good deal," I said enticingly. "You wouldn't have to put up with me."

"Kobie, stop talking nonsense."

Petulantly, I kicked the rungs of the chair.

"If you don't do something about your disposition, you're not going to have a friend in the world," my mother predicted.

"I have a friend. Gretchen. That's all I need."

Other Apple Paperbacks
about Kobie you will enjoy:

*Going on Twelve*

*Thirteen*

*Fourteen and Holding*

*Fifteen at Last*

# ALMOST TEN AND A HALF

## CANDICE F. RANSOM

AN
**APPLE**
PAPERBACK

SCHOLASTIC INC.
New York Toronto London Auckland Sydney

ISBN 0-590-42898-5

12 11 10 9 8 7 6 5 4 3 2                    0 1 2 3 4 5/9

Printed in the U.S.A.                        40

First Scholastic printing, June 1990

*For Linda Shute,*
*who has been on her own*
*for quite some time now*

# 1

The pickax weighed a ton, but I swung it over my head and down again, narrowly missing my foot. The blade hit the iron-hard ground with a faint *ching*, instead of the satisfying *thwack* it made whenever my father swung the pick. A tiny chip of earth flew out of the one-inch trench I was digging.

"Kobie, this is going to take forever," Gretchen said, holding her strawberry-blonde ponytail off her neck.

It was hot for mid-September and even hotter in the woods. My hair wasn't as long as Gretchen's — and it was a plain old brown color — but my neck was sweaty, too.

Propping the pick handle against my leg, I inspected the palms of my hands. I had two blisters about the size of dimes. This was my best idea ever, but it was hard work. Still, nobody said building a roller coaster ride would be a cinch.

"Too bad we don't have two picks," I remarked, wiping my palms on my shorts.

Gretchen slumped down on a stump. "Even if we had fifty picks, we couldn't dig any faster. There's just the two of us."

She unfastened her ponytail clip to pull her hair even higher off her neck. Her blue ponytail clip matched her blouse, and her blouse was almost the same shade of blue as her eyes. I wished I had blue eyes, but mine were plain brown, just like my hair.

"There's always just the two of us," I pointed out. "We're best friends."

"If I had known that digging a ditch was part of being your best friend, I would have signed up as an enemy," Gretchen said dryly.

I knew she didn't mean it. We were both hot and tired, but the project was worth it. Besides, we'd been best friends since second grade. A little thing like digging a two-hundred-yard ditch couldn't affect *our* friendship.

"Are you sure this is going to work?" Gretchen said for about the millionth time.

"Honestly, Gretch. You have no imagination. You look at this hill, and all you see is an old road — "

"A *long* old road."

"I look at this hill, and I see a terrific ride," I went on. "We'll be the only kids in fifth grade with our very own roller coaster. The only kids in Centreville Elementary, for that matter."

The roller coaster ride was my idea, but then,

most of the neat things we did were my ideas.

A few months ago, some men came to cut down trees in the woods next to my house. The men bulldozed a rough road right through the woods, straight up the hill. After they left, I realized the road going down the steep hill could be made into a roller coaster track. I explained it to Gretchen again.

"If we dig a trench just wide enough for the wheels of my scooter, we can ride down the hill without stopping! See, we just push my scooter to the top of the hill, slip the wheels in the track, jump on, and whoosh down the hill! What could be easier?"

"Digging to China." Gretchen crumbled a dry leaf between her fingers.

"It'll be great," I said, trying to drum up a little enthusiasm for my terrific idea. It didn't cost us a thing. The road was already there, the pick belonged to my father, and my old scooter was just rusting away in the shed. All we had to do was apply some elbow grease, as my mother said.

"Elbow grease," I said out loud. "That's all we need."

"Mine are tuckered out," Gretchen sighed.

The trench sure wasn't digging itself. I swung the pick again. The blade bounced off the brick-hard ground, breaking loose a single flake of dirt.

If only it would rain. Sometimes it rained a lot in September, but not this year. We'd had a dry summer, and Dad said we'd probably have a dry fall, too. I lifted the pick once more. Either the pick was getting heavier, or I was getting weaker.

"Is it your turn yet?" I asked Gretchen hopefully.

"I just *had* my turn. You made me dig a whole foot, remember?"

I measured our progress. So far we had dug exactly three feet of track. The distance to the bottom of the hill was about two hundred yards. I'd chipped out maybe an inch. At the rate we were going, we'd be too old to ride down the hill on my scooter. The problem was, we didn't have enough elbows.

Gretchen stood up, brushing leaves off her shorts. She had grown a lot over the summer. Gretchen was taller than I was, but then almost anybody was taller than I was. I hated being short.

"I think my father's here, Kobie. I have to go."

Dropping the pick, I hurried down the hill with Gretchen. We cut through the woods and ran across my backyard. Sure enough, the Farris car was parked in our driveway. Gretchen's father leaned against the fender, talking to my mother.

"Here they are," my mother said as we panted up. "Are you sure Gretchen can't stay for supper? We'd love to have her."

Mr. Farris opened the car door for Gretchen.

4

"Thanks, Mrs. Roberts. But Charles has a game tonight." Charles was Gretchen's older brother.

Gretchen rolled down the window as her father backed the car around. "Bye, Kobie. I had a nice time."

"See you in school tomorrow!" I called. As soon as their car was out of sight, I headed for the woods. Maybe I could dig a few more feet before dark.

"Kobie," my mother said. "Do you have any homework?"

"No. I did my math in the library today."

Actually, I spent about twelve seconds on fractions, and the rest of the time goofing off with Gretchen. I decided that fractions were invented by people who really hated kids. *Nobody* would ever *need* to multiply one third by seven eighths.

"You're sure you don't have any homework?" my mother quizzed. "Last year your teacher told me you only turned in about half your homework."

"Yeah, in arithmetic," I replied, as if that explained why I didn't do it. "After she tattled, I started doing all of it."

"But then you quit turning in your social studies homework," Mom went on. "And when I got after you about that, you did your social studies homework and your arithmetic homework, but you fell down on your history homework."

"Teachers are so unreasonable," I said irritably.

5

"They expect kids to do *everything*."

"I just want to make sure you keep up this year. You ought to be glad I care."

"Mom, I want to work on the hill some more before it gets dark."

"All right," she said. "You can play a while longer. But come when I call you."

I hurried up the logging road before she changed her mind. My mother claimed she cared, but she really only cared about dumb stuff, like whether I did my social studies homework. She didn't give a twig about my important projects. Like the roller coaster. She thought Gretchen and I had been playing all afternoon, instead of doing hard labor.

The last rays of the sun slanted through the trees. I wished Gretchen hadn't gone home. It wasn't much fun digging by myself. Still, it was nice up on the hill. The woods were so quiet —

"Ko-bee! Kobie! Come on in now!" My mother's voice shattered the silence.

Through the trees I could see the back porch of our house. My mother was standing at the rail wearing her old blue sweater. I could see her, but she couldn't see me.

"Kobie Roberts, do you hear me?"

I didn't say a word, hoping she'd give up.

"I know you can hear me," my mother shouted, answering her own question. "Come in the house now."

I didn't want to go in. I hadn't even started digging yet. With only weekends and a couple of hours after school to work, it was taking me forever. I wanted to finish the project before Christmas.

"KOBIE!" Mom bellowed. Now she was getting mad.

*"What!"* I yelled back.

"Come in the house now."

"What for?"

She leaned over the rail and rubbed her back. I knew she was pretty agitated. "If you don't come in right now, I'll tell your father how you wouldn't listen to me!"

That wasn't much of a threat. I hardly ever listened to anybody, unless I absolutely had to, like in school. More than anything in the world, I hated being told what to do.

I threw the pick down in disgust. "All right! I'm coming."

As I walked down the hill, I thought about the book I was reading, *Pippi Longstocking*. Pippi was a girl who didn't take any guff from grownups. She ran her own life, without parents bugging her every five minutes. And she was strong, too. She could lift a horse over her head! I wished Pippi Longstocking lived in Fairfax, Virginia. She'd help me dig that roller coaster trench in no time flat.

My mother was in the kitchen, fixing supper.

7

"I'm here," I said.

She hauled her big mixing bowl from the lower cupboard with a grunt. "Set the table, Kobie. Dad'll be home soon."

"Is that why I had to come in?"

Setting the table was as bad as homework, in my opinion. Stamping over to the cabinets, I yanked the drawer open and grabbed a handful of silverware.

"Forks on the left, knives and spoons on the right," Mom reminded me.

"Why do we have to set the table every night?" I grumbled. "Why can't we just eat right out of the pans, standing over the stove? Then you wouldn't have to wash dishes." And I wouldn't have to dry them.

My mother laughed.

I tossed the silverware on the table, making a terrific clatter. I was hoping Mom would say I was getting on her nerves and tell me to go back outside. She didn't, though. I began dealing knives and forks around the table like playing cards.

When I was little — this was back when I didn't mind being told what to do — I used to love to set the table because I made up stories about each knife, fork, and spoon. None of our silverware matched, so I had an endless supply of stories. The first time I ate at Gretchen's house, I was surprised to see all their silverware was alike. No wonder Gretchen didn't have any imagination.

I had grabbed the fork with U.S.M.C. engraved in the handle. The initials stood for United States Marine Corps. We got the fork at a church picnic. Somebody took our fork by accident and left that one. The U.S.M.C. fork was ugly, so I put it at my mother's place. Served her right for wasting my valuable roller coaster digging time on dumb chores.

"Done," I said. "Can I go back out now?"

"No. It's getting late." She dumped brown sugar into the bowl and mashed margarine into it.

"But I didn't dig hardly any!" I cried.

"Finish tomorrow."

"I *can't* finish tomorrow." Did she honestly think I could build a roller coaster in a day? "I forgot Dad's pick. I left it up on the hill. He won't let me use his tools anymore!"

"You should have thought of that when I called you in," my mother said.

It was then I decided that parents were totally unnecessary. Especially mothers. Didn't Pippi Longstocking get along just fine without *her* parents? And she was the strongest girl in the world besides. I imagined all the things I could do if I suddenly became orphaned. Eat what I wanted, when I wanted, with or without silverware. Stay up late. Build an entire *carnival* in my backyard. And never, ever, be interrupted to do arithmetic or set the table or clean my room.

But I couldn't be an orphan because I still had two parents who were very much alive. I glanced at my mother. She seemed healthy enough, if a little stooped. Maybe I could be a boarder, though.

Inspired with my brilliant new idea, I said, "How about if I pay you and Dad rent?"

Mom added flour to the margarine and sugar mixture. "Rent? What on earth for?"

"So I can live here, but I won't have to be the child. I'll stay in my bedroom and come out for meals. The rest of the time I'll do what I want."

"You do that anyway." Mom stirred a bag of chocolate chips into the bowl.

"It would be a good deal," I said enticingly. "You wouldn't have to put up with me."

"Kobie, stop talking nonsense." She bent to re-trieve the cookie sheets from the cupboard under the sink. "My back is killing me today. Why don't you be still for a while?"

"I don't want to be still," I said petulantly, kick-ing the rungs of the chair. I had been happy up on the hill digging my trench. If she wasn't going to listen to me, she should have let me stay up there.

"If you don't do something about your dispo-sition, you're not going to have a friend in the world," my mother predicted.

"I have a friend. Gretchen. That's all I need." I spun my father's fork around and around. "Actually, I don't even need one friend. I get along fine by myself. I'm almost ten and a half."

"And you think you know everything."

I *did* know a lot. I knew a whole bunch more than when I was just ten. And tons more since I passed ten and a quarter. Imagine how smart I'd be when I reached ten and a half! But nobody took me seriously. Was it any wonder I wanted to be on my own?

"I know I'd be better off without parents," I blurted. "Especially mothers."

My mother stared at me. "What did you say?"

"Nothing," I mumbled. Maybe she didn't hear me.

She did, though. "You know, Kobie, you only have one mother."

"How many mothers does a person need?"

Mom sighed. "Sometimes I wish I still had *my* mother." My grandmother died a long time ago.

Suddenly ashamed, I went over to the counter. "I'll put the cookies on the cookie sheet, Mom. You go sit down and rest your back."

My mother surrendered the spoon. "Remember, twelve cookies on a sheet. And don't put them too close together."

When she left, I dug the spoon into the hill of cookie dough, making a tiny roller coaster track. I put a gob of dough on the cookie sheet, nibbling excess dough off my fingers. Then I licked the spoon. Chocolate chip cookie dough was the yum-

11

miest. It tasted a lot better than cake batter. There was so much dough, it wouldn't hurt to eat some.

When the first cookie sheet was studded with blobs, I started on the other. This cookie sheet was bigger than the one I'd just filled. Obviously it would take more than twelve blobs to fill it, but even then I'd have lots of cookie dough left over. I solved the problem by eating two huge spoonfuls for every spoonful that went on the metal sheet.

"I'm done," I sang out.

My mother came and slipped an oven mitt over her hand. Then she stopped dead at the sight of the empty bowl.

"What happened to the rest of the dough?" she demanded.

"I ate it."

"What?" she cried in exasperation. "Kobie Roberts! You ate the equivalent of four dozen cookies!"

"I did?" It didn't *seem* like four dozen cookies, only a wad of leftover dough.

She glared at me. "I made enough dough for *six dozen* cookies. I thought you were learning fractions. Don't you know how to divide dough to bake cookies in batches?"

"We're not up to that yet," I replied weakly. The dough that had tasted so good going down was not sitting too well on my stomach.

"Well, you'll have to have vanilla wafers in your lunch again this week," Mom declared.

I went into my room without saying anything. I thought she'd appreciate my help. I could have spent the time on my own project. Which just goes to show that you can't satisfy people. Especially parents — double for mothers.

# 2

I should have known my mother wouldn't let me wear baggy red tights and a holey sweater to school, but I tried anyway. It was all part of my experiment.

As soon as I dressed, I went out to the kitchen for my breakfast. My mother took one look at my outfit and said, just as I figured she would, "Kobie, go right back and put on some decent clothes."

"This is what Pippi Longstocking wears," I told her.

"I don't care how your friends dress. No child of mine is going out looking like a ragamuffin."

"Mom, Pippi Longstocking is a character in a book. She wears whatever she feels like putting on that day. Today I feel like wearing this sweater and these tights." My droopy tights were very comfortable. Mom had thrown them away, but I rescued them from the trash. They were still perfectly good.

"You're not going to school like that, Kobie."

"Okay," I said agreeably. "I don't want to go

to school anyway. I'd rather stay home and work on my roller coaster ride."

"That's not what I meant and you know it. Eat, and then go change."

"But there's nothing *wrong* with the way I look," I said. "I'm old enough to pick out my own clothes."

"Clothes, yes. Not rags. Your father works outside all day, and he wears better clothes than you've got on." For his job as foreman of the Grounds Department of Fairfax County Schools, my father wore green pants and a green shirt, to blend in with the grounds, I guess.

My mother plopped bread into the toaster and poured a glass of juice.

"I don't want toast this morning," I said, proceeding to the next stage of my experiment. "I'd like a Hostess Twinkie sundae. With ice cream and chocolate syrup. You can skip the cherry."

"You're getting a fried egg and toast." My mother cracked the egg on the rim of the skillet. "Kids your age need a nutritious breakfast, not junk."

"I'm not a kid," I corrected. "I'm almost ten and a half. I stopped being a kid when I turned ten last summer."

"Is that right?" Mom brought my juice over to the table.

"You didn't shake it, did you?" I asked.

"No. I poured your juice off the top without

shaking it, the way you like it, Your Highness. Heaven forbid you should swallow a little orange pulp."

"Orange pulp, ecchhh! Fish scales, you mean." I sipped the juice cautiously. It looked okay, but I couldn't be too careful. A shred of orange pulp in my juice could ruin my day.

I checked the clock over the sink. Only two minutes had passed since I came out to the kitchen. So far I lost out on everything I wanted to do. I couldn't have a Twinkie sundae for breakfast. I couldn't wear red tights and a holey sweater. And I couldn't stay home from school and work on my roller coaster ride. The experiment turned out just the way I knew it would.

"I think we set a record," I told my mother.

"For what?" She set my plate in front of me.

I stabbed the yolk of my egg. It didn't run. Good. "For not letting me do what I want. Tomorrow I'll bring a list, and you can just cross out everything you won't let me do. Save time."

Sighing, she sat down in my father's chair and rubbed her back. "Kobie, why do you act so spoiled sometimes? When you want to, you can be such a nice little girl."

I ate my egg calmly. I'd heard this complaint a million times, and today I had a ready answer. "Mom, people don't spoil themselves. Somebody has to spoil them."

16

"I suppose your father and I are to blame for your disposition," she remarked.

I didn't want to discuss my rotten disposition. "If you'd just let me do what I want, things would be great around here. I'm old enough to run my own life. Can't you see that? Why don't you let me live here and pretend we're not related?"

"Don't tempt me." Then she became serious. "Kobie, ever since you started fifth grade, you think you're grown up. You aren't, you know. You still have a lot of growing up to do, even if you *are* almost ten and a half."

"Mrs. Victor doesn't think so," I said. "She lets us make our own decisions. She says we are responsible citizens. She doesn't treat me like a baby."

I finished eating, then went back to my room to take off my Pippi Longstocking outfit and put on boring old regular clothes. My mother didn't understand anything. She probably won't let me run my own life, even when I'm almost *forty* and a half.

"What a honker," I exclaimed to Gretchen. We were killing time in the hall outside our class, waiting for the bell to ring. Mr. Breg, the other fifth-grade teacher, had a cold and his nose was red as a beet. "He's getting his handkerchief out. Stand back!"

17

Gretchen nudged me. "Kobie, be quiet. He's only across the hall."

I hurled myself against the wall as Mr. Breg reached into his back pocket and took out a huge square of white cloth. "Look, he pulled the sheet off his bed this morning. If he blows his nose, we'll be knocked over!"

Sure enough, Mr. Breg honked into the handkerchief. He sounded like a flock of wild geese flying south for the winter. I imitated the sound perfectly.

Gretchen giggled helplessly. "Kobie, he'll *hear* us."

"What? What did you say?" I cupped my hand behind my ear. "I'm deaf after that racket."

Mr. Breg frowned at us as he stuffed his handkerchief in his back pocket, where it hung out like a parachute. He was in a bad mood, but then he was always in a bad mood. Talk about a crummy disposition! Compared to grouchy Mr. Breg, I was Rebecca of Sunnybrook Farm.

He guarded the door to his class, across the hall from ours, checking to make sure his students had covered their textbooks. As Gretchen and I watched, Mr. Breg let Debbie Zirk and Donna Storey go inside, but Camille Campbell and a whole bunch of boys were sent to the principal's office.

"Camille told me on the bus they had to have

their books covered by today or else," Gretchen said.

"I wouldn't last five minutes in Breg's class. I'd be in Mr. Leon's office every day." Some boys in Mr. Breg's fifth grade *were* in the principal's office every day. There was probably a special bench for the kids from Mr. Breg's class.

Mr. Breg did everything by the book. Spelling tests every single Friday. A zillion worksheets. Calisthenics during recess. The kids in his class never had any fun.

"We're lucky to have Mrs. Victor," I said to Gretchen.

"She is nice," Gretchen agreed slowly. "But I wish she was more like the other teachers."

I smacked my forehead unbelievingly. "Gretchen! Other teachers are boring! 'Do this, do that,' all day long. Who needs it?"

Just then Lynette O'Bannon came up the hall with Karen Heinz.

"The bell's about to ring," Lynette reported in her whiny voice. "Better get inside."

"Since when do you tell me what to do?" I demanded.

I couldn't stand Lynette O'Bannon. Karen Heinz was so dull she wasn't worth a second glance, but Lynette really got on my nerves.

Lynette's goal in life was to be the teacher's pet. Her favorite subject was tattling. Lynette loved to take names when the teacher left the room. She always volunteered to be the playground monitor so she could order kids around and make them pick up gum wrappers.

Lynette was the kind of kid teachers and parents adored. She was polite and helpful. And she loved to do extra-credit work. So far this year, Lynette had turned in extra reports on Australia, honey bees, and Thomas Jefferson, and school had only started four weeks ago. My mother would have been overjoyed if Lynette O'Bannon suddenly took my place at home. But hard as Lynette tried, she couldn't worm her way into Mrs. Victor's good graces.

Mrs. Victor didn't play favorites. She treated all her students the same. That was one reason why I loved my teacher.

"Did you hear me, Kobie?" Lynette said now, weighted down with library books. Obviously she was slaving over yet another extra-credit report. "The bell is going to ring in about one second."

"So let it ring." I sidled a few inches to the right, blocking the doorway.

Just then the bell shrilled. Mrs. Victor came to the door. "Good morning, girls," she said. "In your seats, okay?"

"Ex-*cuse* me," Lynette said loudly, trying to get Mrs. Victor's attention.

"There's no excuse for you," I quipped.

Mrs. Victor smiled at us as we went into the room.

I was crazy about my teacher. She did things in a nice way. She could have yelled at me for giving Lynette a hard time, but she just reminded us that it was time to begin class. No big deal. If I was in Mr. Breg's class, he probably would have made me crawl on my hands and knees over hot coals to the office to beg forgiveness.

Lynette sashayed ahead to take the desk in front of mine. Gretchen sat next to me, across the aisle. We didn't have assigned seats, but we claimed the same ones every day. Our desks were arranged in short rows in a horseshoe design around the room, with only three desks in a row. Gretchen and I sat in the last row, which meant we could talk without the teacher hearing every word we said, and yet we could still see the board.

At the back of the room were two big tables. Any time we felt like it, we could leave our seats and go sit at the tables. Mrs. Victor didn't mind where we sat, or if we talked, as long as we did our work and were quiet when she was teaching.

"Want to go sit at the table?" I asked Gretchen.

"Okay," she answered hesitantly. I could tell she really didn't, though. Gretchen preferred to sit at her desk. I think she felt safe there.

"We'll stay here," I said, stowing my notebook in the cubby under my desk.

Gretchen flashed me a grateful look. Then she slid her books under her desk, leaving her notebook on top. I glanced at her notebook with envy.

The notebook was a new style called a Nifty. Instead of finger-pinching rings, the Nifty had a magnetic strip that held looseleaf sheets. The notebook was flat, and the cover folded back. Best of all were the secret compartments under the magnetic strip — a long, narrow one for pencils, and smaller ones for lunch money and erasers.

I was dying to have a Nifty notebook, but they cost too much my mother said, and there wasn't anything wrong with my ring binder. There *was* something wrong with my binder. The rings pinched that flap of skin between my thumb and index finger every time I opened it. Even if I came home black and blue and crippled for life, my mother wouldn't buy me a Nifty like Gretchen's. My mother believed in using things until they fell apart. I pictured myself at forty and a half, paddling my scooter to work and carrying my same dumb ring-binder.

"What's that?" I said, pointing to a colored sheet sticking out of Gretchen's notebook.

She pulled out a map and passed it to me. "I heard we're supposed to study the United States this year. All fifth-graders have to learn the state capitals. I thought I'd get ready."

I handed the map back to her, uninterested. "Mrs. Victor will probably give us a choice."

"I hope she just tells us what to do. I don't want to make any more choices."

"Gretchen, that's the best part of this class," I said. "We don't have to do anything we don't really want to. Mrs. Victor says we're old enough to make our own decisions."

"That's all right for you, Kobie, but I'd rather be told what we're going to do. I don't like wondering about things."

"You'd rather be treated like a baby instead of a real person?" I took out a fresh piece of paper and began sketching Mr. Breg, giving him a nose like a moose's.

"It's the teacher's job to tell us what to do," Gretchen insisted. "At least we still have to do stuff like arithmetic and reading. We don't have a choice in *every*thing, Kobie."

"Too bad." I didn't mind reading, but arithmetic was a total drag. In my entire lifetime, I never planned to use fractions.

I showed Gretchen my drawing. "Honestly, Kobie," she commented with a giggle. "You're terrible. You'll use up all your paper before class starts."

"So? Mom will buy me some more when she goes to the store." But my mother was already complaining that she had to buy me a new pack of paper every week. I didn't use *all* my paper on drawings — I saved a few sheets for homework.

Mrs. Victor called roll. After the flag salute,

she announced we'd begin the day with music, because it was Wednesday. Every Wednesday we had either art or music.

I hated music. Singing was nice, but we didn't do that in fifth grade. We played musical instruments instead. The instruments were really dumb — wooden blocks and triangles and spoons. We had a tambourine and a xylophone, but only one of each so we had to take turns. With twenty-eight kids in our class, I'd probably never have a turn at either the tambourine or the xylophone. And my idea of fun wasn't plinking a triangle or whacking two wooden blocks together.

Before she gave out the instruments, Mrs. Victor said, "Does anyone not feel like music today? Who would like to go to the library?"

My hand was already in the air. "We don't," I told the teacher. "Gretchen and I want to go to the library."

"Kobie and Gretchen. Anyone else?"

Vincent Wheatly and Richard Supinger both raised their hands. Vincent and Richard were the class troublemakers. They could carry on in the library easier than they could in class. Lynette O'Bannon and her friend Karen Heinz decided to go, too. Mrs. Victor wrote out six library passes.

"Come on," I urged Gretchen, who still hadn't packed up her things.

She pursed her lips. "I never said I wanted to go to the library."

"You'd rather stay here and play 'Row, Row, Row Your Boat' with wooden blocks? At least we'll have fun in the library."

Sighing, Gretchen piled her spelling book on her notebook and followed me out of the room.

Lynette and Karen were just ahead of us. Lynette walked like a duck, carefully placing her foot in the center of each linoleum tile.

"Let's pass these slowpokes," I said to Gretchen, speeding up.

" 'Step on a crack, break your mother's back. Step on a line, break your mother's spine,' " Lynette chanted as we breezed by. "Boy, Kobie, you must really want to hurt your mother. Look at all the lines you're stepping on."

That girl always managed to get my goat. "I'm going to step all over your face, O'Bannon. Take your baby games someplace else."

"No running in the hall. I'm telling!" she squawked.

"You always tattle. That's why nobody likes you."

"You're a great one to talk," Lynette retorted. "If Gretchen didn't like you, you wouldn't have a friend in the world, Kobie Roberts."

But I hurried down the hall, deliberately stepping on all the lines I could.

Gretchen ran to catch up with me. "Kobie, you didn't have to be so mean to Lynette."

"She started it, Gretchen. She knows I can't

25

stand to be on the same planet with her, and she always says stuff to make me mad."

"I think she'd like to be friends," Gretchen said thoughtfully. "Maybe if you were nice to her, she'd be nice to you."

I snorted. "I don't need Lynette for a friend. I'm not that desperate."

"You never give her a chance," Gretchen said. "You never give anybody a chance, really."

"Why are people always telling me how to be?" I asked. "My mother tells me I have a rotten disposition. And now you tell me to be nice to the class creep. Why can't people just let me be myself?"

"You never want to be like anybody else," Gretchen pointed out. "It's like you're in a private club or something. You always have to be different, Kobie."

"No, I don't," I argued. "I'm just me. This is the way I am. Just plain old Kobie."

Actually, I wasn't plain old Kobie. I *was* different. A little outrageous, like Pippi Longstocking. I was special, too, though it wasn't the sort of thing I could work naturally into a casual conversation. "By the way, have you ever noticed how special I am?"

"Sometimes I think you don't need anybody," Gretchen said.

Absorbed in the book display outside the library, I didn't reply.

# 3

I planned to work on my roller coaster ride as soon as I got home from school, but my mother had other ideas.

"Come look at your room," she said, leading me back through the house.

I followed reluctantly, thinking she'd found something in there she wasn't supposed to, like the snakeskin I was drying on the box springs under my mattress. A few weeks ago, she made me throw out my bird's nest collection because she said the nests had lice.

Now my mother opened the door grandly, as if it were the gateway to Disneyland. My room *did* look different. It was clean, really clean! No clothes on the floor, no drawings peeking out from under the bed. Even the rocks on my bookcase had been lined up neatly. All my barrettes and hair ribbons had been sorted out and put in a new plastic tray on my dresser.

"It looks great," I said with wonder. "All of it." Usually, when I cleaned my messy room, I only did one part of it, like make the bed.

"I worked all day in here," my mother said, rubbing her back with one hand. "This place was worse than any hogpen. I don't know how you let it get such a mess, Kobie."

"You did a good job," I said cheerfully. The whole house sparkled with Mom's fall cleaning.

"I straightened all your dresser drawers but the bottom one. It hurts my back to stoop that low. I want you to clean it out."

"Now?"

"Now." She wiped a speck of dust off my bookcase. With that grim I-want-everything-spotless look on her face, I was surprised the dust didn't jump off the furniture itself.

"But, Mom!" I protested. "That's my junk drawer. It's not *supposed* to be neat."

"It's not supposed to be so loaded down you can't open it, either," she countered. "I'll bring you a bag to put trash in."

"But I want to go outside and work on my roller coaster track." Just because *she* was on a neatness kick, I couldn't do what I wanted to. I didn't *ask* her to clean my room. It was fine the way it was. That was the trouble with parents, they meddled too much. Especially mothers.

"If you hurry, you can still go out." She left to get me a trash bag.

Resigned, I sat down on the floor and braced my feet against my dresser. Then I tugged at the bottom drawer until it opened with a slow *skreeeek*, like the sound of a board being pried loose with a crowbar. Instead of sliding out, the drawer crashed to the floor with a thud. Books and papers spewed all over the rug.

Tilting the drawer so everything spilled out on the floor, I began sorting through piles of drawings, old homework papers (which went immediately into the trash bag), comic books, and art supplies.

My art supplies were pathetic. None of my crayons had wrappers and my colored pencils were the cheap kind that barely left a mark on paper. I longed for a new box of crayons, the sixty-four kind with colors like blue-green and magenta and copper which smelled like pennies.

Every sheet of paper had been scribbled on. My greatest wish — aside from not having any parents — was to own an unlimited supply of paper. And a Nifty notebook.

When I had finished sorting, I put the good stuff back in the drawer. I could actually close it without straining. It *was* kind of nice having a completely clean room, but I would rather have been working on my roller coaster ride.

I dragged the trash bag out to the laundry porch. "I'm going out now," I told my mother, who was in the kitchen frying hamburgers.

"Not now, Kobie. *Listen* to me! Your father just got home and supper's almost ready."

"You *promised* I could go out if I cleaned my

29

bottom drawer!" I exploded. "Now you tell me I can't! That's not fair!"

"Who said life was fair?"

Peeved, I went outside to meet my father. His old green pick-up chugged and coughed as he shut the engine off.

"You're late," I remarked as my father climbed down from the cab.

"I know. I had to go back to Oak Hill School. Some kid threw a manhole cover down the sewer and guess who had to retrieve it before somebody fell into the manhole and got hurt."

Usually Dad and his crew of workers mowed school yards or built baseball diamonds. But sometimes he had emergency calls, like finding manhole covers. One time he had to rescue a cat that was trapped in a school's furnace room.

Now Dad plopped his cap on my head and reached across the seat for his lunchbox, which he handed to me.

"Did you leave me anything?" I asked.

"You might find a candy bar in there." A lot of times he didn't eat the dessert Mom packed.

I unlatched his lunch box and took out the Oh Henry! bar. "Thanks, Dad. I'm starving. I didn't even have a snack today. Mom made me clean out my dresser drawer as soon as I got home. She sure is grouchy lately."

We walked up to the house together. I matched my steps with Dad's long strides.

"Go easy on your mother," Dad said as we went inside. "She doesn't feel well these days. As a matter of fact, we've got some news to tell you."

"What?" Maybe they were going to let me pay room and board after all. Maybe they were finally fed up having me as their child.

"Let your mother get supper on the table first. Then we'll talk, okay?" Dad went over to kiss my mother on the cheek. I put his lunchbox on the counter.

"Wash your hands, Kobie," Mom said wearily.

I followed Dad into the bathroom. He lathered his hands with his beige scrubbing soap, then took my hands in his so mine got soapy, too. "Don't rub too hard," Dad advised. "That soap will take the skin off."

"I'm tough," I told him. "See my calluses from digging my roller coaster track?"

Our plates were on the table when we went back to the kitchen. I sat down in my place and immediately lifted the bun of my hamburger to make sure it was the way I liked it.

"The special sauce is on there," Mom said. "And your hamburger is extra-flat."

"Two pickle chips in the middle?" I asked.

"Two pickle chips, dead center."

Satisfied that everything was in order, I took a big bite. Then I raised the bun again and removed the pickle chips before I accidently bit into them. I laid them on the edge of my plate, where

31

I always put yucky foods I wasn't going to eat.

My father stared at me over his own hamburger. "Kobie, what are you doing?"

"Taking out the pickles."

"Don't you want pickles? You just asked if they were on there."

"I want pickles on my hamburger," I explained. "But I don't want to eat them."

"You put pickles on her hamburger so she can pick them off?" Dad asked my mother.

Mom smiled at my father's confusion. "Kobie likes her hamburger the way they fix them at McDonald's. So I fry her patty thin and make that special pink sauce. And I put two pickles on it, just the way McDonald's does."

"But I never eat them," I said. "Pickles are gross. They look like lizards that got run over by a car."

Now Mom frowned. "That's enough, Kobie. We don't talk about such things at the table."

"But it's true. Don't you think pickle chips look like run-over lizards, Dad?" I rattled on, thinking of all the foods I couldn't stand to look at, much less eat. "And raisins. Don't raisins remind you of squished bugs? I can't stand grapes, either. They're just like eyeballs — "

"Kobie!" My mother was really angry now. "If you can't say anything nice, don't say anything at all."

I chewed my hamburger thoughtfully. "But

Mom, I'd never get to talk. The best stuff isn't nice. That's what makes it interesting. If you talk about nice things all the time, people get bored."

"Kobie." Dad spoke in a warning tone. "Your mother has something to tell you."

I'd forgotten about the important discussion we were going to have at dinner. "What's up, Mom?"

My mother wiped her lips with her napkin. "I have to go to an orthopedic hospital, Kobie."

"Hospital?" I screeched. "Are you sick? How come nobody told me? What's the matter with you?"

"We're telling you now. I only found out for certain today," Mom said. "I'm having traction, for my back. The doctor will use weights and pulleys to straighten the disks in my back. It's a slow process but my doctor thinks it'll be better than having surgery. When I come home, my back won't hurt anymore."

"How long will you be gone?" I asked.

"Several weeks," she replied. "I might not be home until Thanksgiving."

I thought about this. My mother was going to the hospital! She was acting pretty cool about it. I don't know if I'd be so calm. I wouldn't like weights pulling on my back, unless it would make me grow taller. My mother was awfully brave.

Then I thought of something else. With Mom in the hospital, I'd be an orphan! Well, half an orphan. During the day, while Dad was at work, I'd be on my own, though. This was better than being a boarder. I'd get to come and go as I pleased, without paying rent.

My mother minced her french fries into mashed potatoes. She was probably worrying about me staying here all alone.

"I'll be fine," I said, to put her mind at ease. "Have a good time at the hospital and don't worry about me."

Dad finished his hamburger, then pushed his plate away. "We've hired a housekeeper, Kobie. She'll cook and clean and take care of you while your mother is in the hospital."

A housekeeper! How could I be on my own with a housekeeper hovering around?

"I don't need a housekeeper," I said. "I'm independent."

"What about me?" Dad asked. "Who's going to cook supper and clean the house? I work all day, remember?"

"I'll do it," I offered. "I'll cook and clean and take care of us. I can make toast."

He exchanged a smile with my mother. "It's a big job, Kobie. You go to school. How would you have time to cook and clean?"

"I'll skip school until Mom comes home," I suggested hopefully.

Dad quickly scorched that notion. "We've already hired the housekeeper."

"You'll like Mrs. Blevins," Mom told me. "She's very nice."

34

I wouldn't be half an orphan with a busybody housekeeper around. I decided I'd better let this Mrs. Blevins know how things were to be right off. Dad hired her to cook and clean — she wouldn't have anything to do with me.

I looked at my mother. "When are you leaving for the hospital?"

"Sunday," she replied.

So soon! My stomach quivered uncertainly the way it did when it was my turn in the dentist's chair.

"I thought you could visit Gretchen that afternoon, while your father takes me to the hospital," Mom continued. "Then he'll pick up Mrs. Blevins on his way home."

"Can't I go to the hospital with you?" I'd never been in a hospital before. It sounded interesting, blood and guts and sick people.

"I'm sorry, Kobie, but they don't allow children under the age of twelve in the patients' rooms. You'd have to wait in the lobby downstairs. I don't want you to be alone that long."

"I'll be okay," I said confidently. "I'm almost ten and a half, you know."

"Even so," Mom said, "it won't be much fun sitting in a lobby."

I really wasn't used to the idea of my mom being in the hospital yet. "Can I go outside now?" I asked. "I'm through eating."

Dad rose to collect his and my mother's plates.

"Run along, Kobie. I'll help your mother with the dishes tonight. Don't stay out too long. It'll be dark soon."

"Take your jacket," Mom said. "And come when I call you this time."

I raced across the yard and into the woods, my jacket flapping behind me as I tied it around my waist. Scrambling up the side of the bank, I tore through brambles and briars to the logging road.

My father's pick was lying where I left it. The roller coaster track looked even shorter than I remembered, a few feet of crumbly crooked ditch.

Standing tall, I gazed through the trees to the other side of our property. The sun was getting ready to sink beneath the distant Blue Ridge mountains. Shadows cast by the clothesline poles stretched across our lawn like gigantic storks.

I liked this time of day, when everything was dusky and purple. Sitting on the stump, I thought about my mother's trip to the hospital. She wouldn't be home for weeks — maybe not till Thanksgiving. That was a long time to be without a mother. The quivery, uncertain feeling started in my stomach again. Then I remembered I'd be independent all those weeks.

When my mother came back, she'd see how well I did on my own. She would have to agree that I was capable of running my life. The long separation would be worth it.

Off to one side, I saw something hop. Barely

turning my head, I spied a tiny brown rabbit loping down the road, heading in my direction. I remained still. The rabbit didn't see me.

I held my breath. In all the times I'd been up on this hill, I've never been this close to an animal before. I'd always wanted a wild animal pet, especially a baby one. Pippi Longstocking had a tame monkey. Now was *my* chance.

Luckily there was no wind this evening. The rabbit hadn't caught my scent yet. Moving very slowly, I untied my jacket from around my waist and held it out in front of me.

The rabbit stopped suddenly and sat up on its haunches, twitching its nose. It knew a human was there. I had to act fast.

Lunging forward, I threw the jacket out in front of me like a net. I fell to my knees and pinned the edges of the jacket with my arms.

A small hump in the middle of my jacket told me I had captured the rabbit. He hadn't run away! He was under my jacket, so scared I could detect his heartbeat through the material.

Excitement fluttered in my stomach. I had actually caught a wild animal with my bare hands! I was dying to peer under the jacket and say hi to my new pet, but I was afraid he'd run out. He might even bite me. Dad had warned me a thousand times about rabbits and squirrels and other animals that lived in the woods. They all had razor-sharp teeth and sometimes carried rabies.

Then a thought struck me. How would I get my rabbit home? As soon as I raised the jacket, he'd scoot off like lightning. If I reached my hand inside, he'd bite me for sure. And if I picked up my jacket with the rabbit wrapped in it, I might hurt him. He was just a baby.

Kneeling in the dirt with my rump up in the air, I felt sort of ridiculous. I couldn't move. Both the rabbit and I were pinned to the ground. Even if I somehow managed to get the rabbit home, what would I do with it? No way would Mom let me keep it in my room. Dad wouldn't be able to build a pen for it until the weekend, and anyway, I knew he wouldn't like the idea. Wild animals belonged in the wild, he always said.

What could I do?

At last I did the only thing that was left. I got up and carefully lifted my jacket. The dazed bunny squatted motionless for a few seconds, then scampered into the brush with a flick of his white tail.

The sun had just about dipped behind the trees. Any second my mother would come out on the porch and yell for me to come home. I draped my jacket over my shoulder and began hiking down the logging road.

Freeing the bunny was the right thing, I told myself. But still, it felt really strange to get something I'd wanted all my life, and then let it go.

# 4

"Give me all your . . . sevens," Gretchen said, fanning her hand of cards.

I checked my cards, even though I knew I didn't have any sevens. "Go fish," I said sourly. Gretchen was beating the pants off me.

Gretchen drew a card off the top of the deck. Her face lit up. "I got what I wanted," she crowed, showing me the seven of spades. "My turn again." She laid the four sevens on the bed with the rest of her sets of matched cards, then said, "Give me all your kings."

With a sigh of disgust, I tossed her the two kings I'd been saving. "I'm tired of playing. Let's do something else."

Gretchen counted her sets of cards. "You don't want to play because you're losing. You do this every time, Kobie. Quit when I'm winning."

"I do not," I said, flinging the rest of my cards on the bed. "I'm just tired of cards, that's all. I wish we could go out."

All weekend I'd been excited about spending

the afternoon with Gretchen. We planned to explore an old abandoned shack up the road from her house. I was sure that counterfeiters were holed up in the shack with their printing press. We were going to hide in the bushes until the counterfeiters went out for a newspaper or something, then run in and snitch a few fifties and hundreds that were probably drying on the clothesline.

Then it started raining, about five minutes after my father dropped me off at Gretchen's house. Mrs. Farris fixed us grilled cheese and bacon sandwiches and tomato soup. She always made whatever we wanted to eat. But she wouldn't let us go outside, not even when I told her I'd make it worth her while.

"You'll catch your death in the pouring rain, both of you," she cautioned, never realizing she was passing up an easy fifty bucks. "I'm sure you don't want to get sick and worry your mother, Kobie. She's got enough on her mind."

After lunch, we went into Gretchen's room to wait for the rain to stop. Only the storm didn't seem like it would ever let up. We sat on the bed and played cards while the rain fell in buckets. I wouldn't have liked the day any better if I *had* been winning.

With another sigh, I dumped the paper bag on Gretchen's pillow and sorted sullenly through the contents. On our way to Gretchen's house, my father stopped at George's Store so I could buy candy for me and Gretchen to share.

Gretchen gathered the scattered cards. "What's left?"

"A million wrappers and six licorice Neccos. Want one?"

She wrinkled her nose. "How come they put so many licorice ones in? Nobody ever eats them."

I pawed through the wrappers, hoping to unearth an overlooked Tootsie Roll. "If this rain keeps up, we ought to start building an ark."

"I wonder what she's doing?" Gretchen mused, straightening the cards into a neat square.

"Who?"

"Who? Your *mother*, Kobie. How often does your mother go to the hospital?"

"I guess maybe she's in bed wearing that funny gown she told me about. The one with no back they make you wear in the hospital," I replied. "Dad said first they'd have to sign some papers. Then Mom has to go to bed right away. I would have gone with them, but I didn't feel like sitting in the lobby all that time."

"I bet you miss her already," Gretchen said softly.

"Miss who?"

"Oh, Kobie. I don't know why you pretend to be so terrible."

"Who's pretending?" Sliding off the bed, I went over to the window, hoping to spot a break in the

41

clouds. "I made her a card to open after Dad leaves. I'm going to call her tonight and ask her how she likes it."

"I'm sure she'll love it."

It *was* a pretty neat card. I drew a picture of my mother in bed hooked up to a bunch of pulleys and weights. On the front I wrote, "Don't hang around too long." And inside I put, "Hurry home soon." The traction looked sort of like a hangman's noose, but I hoped Mom would understand what it was supposed to be.

Before Dad drove me to Gretchen's house, I kissed Mom good-bye and gave her the card. She smelled like Johnson's baby powder. She told me to be a good girl and hugged me so hard I could hardly breathe. There were tears in her eyes as she watched me skip out the door. I was so happy to be going to Gretchen's I didn't realize, until this minute, that my mother was crying because she wouldn't see me again until she came home.

"She'll be gone for weeks," I told Gretchen. "She might not be home until Thanksgiving." Since it was still September, Thanksgiving seemed like a year away.

"That's a long time. But you'll have a baby-sitter."

"Housekeeper," I corrected staunchly. "She just cooks and cleans the house."

"Housekeeper, then," Gretchen repeated. "When is she coming?"

"Dad's picking her up after he takes Mom to the hospital. Then he'll come get me."

"Do you know anything about her?" Gretchen asked.

I shook my head. "Only that she's supposed to be nice. And kind of old, I think." Secretly I pictured a gray-haired maid in a uniform who called me "Miss Roberts" or maybe even "ma'am" and brought me Twinkie sundaes on a silver tray.

"As old as Mrs. Settinger?"

"I hope not!" Mrs. Settinger was the cafeteria lady at school who yelled at the kids to hurry through the serving line. Mrs. Settinger was so mean, little kids had nightmares about her. Maybe the housekeeper *wouldn't* be nice. Maybe she'd be horrible.

"She won't be like Mrs. Settinger," Gretchen reassured me. "Nobody could be that awful."

But the image of the gray-haired maid suddenly vanished and in its place a gruesome picture formed in my mind.

"I bet she has big rowboat feet," I said. "And warts on her chin. With hairs sticking out."

"Long fangs!" Gretchen added, giggling. "And her eyes are crossed!"

"No! She only has *one* eye," I cried. "She wears an eye patch to cover up the empty socket. She only takes the patch off at night, and if anybody ever saw her, they'd be grossed out!"

"Ewwwww!" Gretchen squealed, burying her

43

face in her pillow. "Kobie, you *are* terrible!"

I laughed. Even if Mrs. Blevins had *three* eyes, all of them bloodshot, I didn't care. It really didn't matter if she was nice or not, as long as she let me do as I pleased.

As it turned out, Mrs. Blevins had bright blue eyes and no eye patches. She did not have any warts with hairs sticking out, at least not where I could see them. She did not have fangs or feet like rowboats.

In fact, Mrs. Blevins had the sweetest face I'd ever seen, with soft pink skin and dimples. Her snowy hair was piled on top of her head like whipped cream. She had glasses made of thin silvery wires. Over her dumpling shape, she wore a white apron and a dress printed with blue flowers. Mrs. Blevins looked like a fairy-tale grandmother, an over-the-river-and-through-the-woods type of grandmother.

I wasn't sure she was real.

Before Dad stopped the car, the side door opened and Mrs. Blevins came down the steps, smiling warmly at me.

"You must be Kobie," Mrs. Blevins said as I got out of the car. "How are you, dear?"

I glanced around to make sure there wasn't anyone else around with my name. Nobody ever called me "dear," unless I was sick or something.

44

My father prodded me. "Kobie, can't you speak?"

Mrs. Blevins kindly defended my lapse in manners. "She's just shy, aren't you, Kobie?"

"Kobie has never been shy a day in her life," my father stated, opening the trunk of our car and taking out two suitcases. "Kobie, this little one isn't heavy. Carry it into the spare bedroom for Mrs. Blevins so she can finish unpacking. And show her where things are."

Well, this was a switch! I expected Mrs. Blevins to carry *my* stuff, not the other way around. Dad obviously didn't understand the rules, either. After all, we'd never had a housekeeper before.

I picked up the small suitcase and took it into the house. In the spare bedroom, which was next to mine, I dropped the suitcase on the floor. Mrs. Blevins followed me into the room.

I noticed she had already unpacked a lot of stuff. Pictures in frames on the nightstand table. A silver brush and comb set on the dresser. Fluffy slippers by the rocking chair. Mrs. Blevins was here to stay.

My father brought in the second suitcase. "If you need anything," he told Mrs. Blevins, "just yell for Kobie."

Yell for Kobie! Who was the housekeeper around here?

When he left, I said, "I might not be around. I'm very busy, you know."

"I'm sure you are. Would you like to see my great-grandchildren?" Mrs. Blevins asked me. "I have five. They are so sweet. I take their pictures everywhere I go."

"Must get awfully heavy," I murmured as I stared into the frames. Two buck-toothed little boys, two little girls with bangs that separated into a v on their foreheads. The last photograph was of a pumpkin-headed baby with googly eyes and a wet bib.

Laughing, Mrs. Blevins dusted the baby's picture with the hem of her apron.

I cleared my throat. "Mrs. Blevins, I think you should know that I'm not an ordinary kid. I'm very independent."

"Oh, I can tell you're very grown-up," she said, hanging some dresses in the closet. "How old are you, Kobie? Twelve?"

She thought I was twelve! Maybe we should have gotten a housekeeper sooner.

"Almost ten and a half," I admitted. "But I'm on my own. I just live here."

Her silvery glasses flashed. "I see."

"I come and go as I please," I explained, just in case she missed the point.

"Really? And your parents let you?" she inquired with the tiniest hint of disbelief.

" . . . Mostly."

Mrs. Blevins folded sweaters into a drawer. "Where do you go to school, Kobie?"

"Centreville Elementary. But only for a little while. I'm just going to make my parents happy. They want me to learn fractions. As soon as I do, I'm quitting."

I thought she was smiling, but I couldn't be sure. "Sometimes it takes a while to catch on. I had trouble with fractions, myself."

Her unpacking completed, Mrs. Blevins turned to me. "Kobie, I hope we can become friends. Since I'm new at this job, maybe you could tell me when you leave and where you're going — just at first, until I get used to the routine around here."

That seemed fair enough. "Well, I mostly go up on the hill in the woods. I'm working on a secret project," I said, hoping she'd ask what it was. But she didn't. "I'll let you know when I go out. Just at first."

"Good." She smiled. "And if you get stuck with your fractions homework, I'll be glad to help."

Mrs. Blevins really *was* nice, as my mother had promised. I could afford to be generous and show her the ropes, now that we understood one another.

"Uh, the bathroom is down the hall. You have to jiggle the handle when you flush the toilet or else the pump keeps running."

Mrs. Blevins smiled at me gratefully. "Thank you, Kobie."

My mother had cooked a ham before she left.

We had that plus baked beans and biscuits for supper. Mrs. Blevins sat in my mother's chair. Mrs. Blevins could have taken the extra chair against the wall, but I suppose she needed to be able to jump up and get things for us. I don't know why, but it irked me to see her in my mother's chair.

Mrs. Blevins wanted to hear every detail about my mother's ailment. She clucked her tongue sympathetically as my father related Mom's back problem. Then he said how much Mom liked the card I made her.

"You drew your mother a card?" Mrs. Blevins asked, as if I'd painted the Mona Lisa. "Kobie is so thoughtful and sweet."

I caught my father's eye across the table. I knew he was thinking that "sweet" wasn't the way people usually described me.

When we were through eating, Dad said, "Kobie, help Mrs. Blevins clear the table."

"Oh, I can do it." Mrs. Blevins dismissed any mention of assistance with a wave. "Kobie can run along if she wants."

Dad wouldn't hear of it. "It's Kobie's job to clear the table and dry the dishes."

"But, Dad — "

Mrs. Blevins bustled past with the bean casserole. "Let the child go. I can manage, Mr. Roberts."

"Yeah. Let the child go," I echoed.

Unwilling to argue in front of a stranger, Dad said, "All right, Kobie. You're free tonight."

Mrs. Blevins carried a stack of plates to the counter. She winked at me, as if to say I could forget about doing the dishes as long as she was here. Which was fine with me.

Humming, I went to call my mother and see how she'd liked my card. After I talked to her I headed into the living room and switched on the TV. I watched my favorite programs nonstop. Mrs. Blevins didn't pester me about doing my homework or anything. She even brought me a piece of pie, warmed, with a scoop of ice cream. And she let me eat in the living room. My mother practically had me arrested if I walked into the living room with a potato chip in my hand.

At nine o'clock I turned the TV off. My father was reading the paper in his red leather chair. Mrs. Blevins sat on the sofa, knitting something white and lacy.

"Well," I announced casually. "I guess I'll go to bed."

"Not already!" Mrs. Blevins exclaimed. "Surely you can stay up a little longer."

I was all for it. "Dad?"

He folded his newspaper with a crackle. "I'm afraid not, Kobie. It's a school night. Nine o'clock is your regular bedtime."

I wished he hadn't said that — Mrs. Blevins thought I was on my own. Independent people did not go to bed at nine o'clock unless they wanted to.

In my room, I changed into my nightgown, then arranged my stuffed animals on my bed. All twenty-seven stuffed animals slept with me, and it took a while to line them up.

Someone knocked on my door. Mrs. Blevins poked her smiling face inside. "You're in your nightie already. My, that's quite a collection of teddy bears."

"They aren't all bears," I said. "In fact, I only have four bears." I placed Ellsworth, my favorite elephant, up by my pillow, then slid between the covers.

Mrs. Blevins came over to pull the blankets under my chin. "Good night, Kobie. See you in the morning."

When my mother tucked me in, she always said this silly little rhyme. "Good night, sleep tight, and don't let the bedbugs bite." Corny, but I was used to hearing it.

But Mrs. Blevins didn't say anything else. She closed the door softly behind her. I had to get up and open it a crack, so a slice of light from the hall fell across the foot of my bed. My mother never closed the door all the way. She knew I didn't like total darkness.

I crawled back in bed, but I had a hard time getting comfortable. Even after moving Barney the Panda and Dixie Mouse, I didn't feel sleepy.

I lay awake, wondering if the light from the hospital hall fell across my mother's bed.

I was on my own, for real. I'd have to tuck myself in from now on. In a whisper, I recited to myself, "Good night, sleep tight, and don't let the bedbugs bite."

Then I went to sleep.

# 5

When Mrs. Victor wasn't looking, I put my hand on the rubber mat of the enlarging machine. A giant-sized version of my right hand appeared on the paper beside the mat. I wiggled my fingers. My hand looked huge, strong. A hand that could do anything. If the rest of me matched my right hand, I could lift a horse, like Pippi Longstocking.

"Mrs. Vic-tor, Kobie's got her hand in the enlarging machine," Lynette O'Bannon sang loudly.

I pulled my hand out and gave Lynette a black look. Tattletale.

Mrs. Victor didn't like tattletales, either. Instead of yelling at me, she just clapped to get our attention and said, "Get your pictures ready, class."

I went back to the table, tromping on Lynette's foot as I walked past.

"Mrs. Victor," Lynette squeaked, but the teacher was busy setting up the machine.

Gretchen didn't see what I had done. She anxiously leafed through a book of flowers. "Do you think this one is okay?" she asked me, pointing to a picture of a red poppy.

"Yeah, it's fine. Just copy it and then start on your sand painting," I told her.

"I can't copy this picture, Kobie, I'll have to use the machine to make it bigger so I can trace it."

"Not me." I opened my library book, *Stamps of the World*, to the page I had marked. "I'm doing this one."

Gretchen gaped at the photograph. "Gosh, Kobie. That stamp is so small. It'll take you forever to draw it freehand."

"No, it won't." I angled the book so I could copy the bird stamp on the piece of cardboard the teacher gave each of us. Confidently, I began sketching the fern the bird was perched on.

Lynette and Karen stopped by our table on their way up to the machine. "Let me see which one you're doing," Lynette asked Gretchen, deliberately ignoring me.

Gretchen showed her the poppy picture. "Are you doing that horse? That'll be really neat. Kobie's drawing hers freehand."

Lynette poked her nosy self over my shoulder. "It'll be awfully hard to make a sand painting out of that itty-bitty stamp," she pronounced.

"Who dialed your number?" I said sarcastically. "How come you aren't drawing your horse freehand, Lynette? A terrific artist like you."

Actually, Lynette was a fair artist. Not as good as me, but better than the rest of the fifth graders. Too bad she had a personality problem. Once in a while, I wished I had somebody to talk to about art. Gretchen was a terrific friend, but she didn't like art at all. I would have to be crazy, though, to want Lynette O'Bannon for a friend.

"I want to make sure *my* picture comes out exact," Lynette said.

"If you say so." I patted back a fake yawn. "You guys better hurry. Looks like quite a crowd up there." Let the others stand in line like sheep. I felt good drawing my picture freehand, on my own, without an enlarging machine.

By the time Gretchen returned with her flower picture penciled on her piece of cardboard, I had finished my drawing.

"I'll get our supplies," I said.

"I need bright red and two kinds of green," said Gretchen.

Mrs. Victor had set out several cans of tempera powder and a big box of fine white sand. I put a little of each color of tempera powder in baby food jar lids. Then I shoveled sand into a plastic baggie. On a tray, I added a bunch of Popsicle sticks, a wooden paddle, and a jar of white glue. I gave Gretchen the jar lids containing red and green tempera powder.

She regarded the supplies with dismay. "I don't know how to do this."

54

"It's easy. Just mix a little sand with the powder," I instructed. "When you stir it enough, it'll look like colored sand." I arranged my jar lids of tempera powder in a semi-circle and began spooning sand into each one.

Gretchen sighed as she stirred sand into her red jar lid with a wooden stick. "I wish Mrs. Victor would forget about art. I'd rather do reading or even spelling than make these dumb pictures."

"You could have gone to the library," I reminded her. "You had a choice."

"I know, but you stayed. I didn't want to go to the library by myself."

I always stayed in the room on Art Wednesdays. Mrs. Victor's projects were fun and not at all like boring old music.

"Art is a million times better than music," I said, scornfully tapping "Row, Row, Row Your Boat" on the table top with my spoon. "At least it's creative."

"For you, maybe," Gretchen allowed. "For me, it's work. No matter how hard I try, my pictures never look good."

Sometimes I didn't understand Gretchen. She really hated creative time, unless the teacher told her exactly what to make. Whenever the teacher handed out big sheets of paper and let us draw whatever we wanted — my favorite thing in the world to do — I practically pounced on my paper and began drawing something complicated, like a scene from Africa. I almost always ran out of time.

But Gretchen just sat there with her pencil loose in her fingers and a miserable expression on her face.

"I can't think of anything," she'd admit in a low voice.

I'd stare at her. How could she not be able to think of *any*thing? My head was always crammed with ideas and projects and pictures I wanted to draw. My problem was, I never had enough paper.

"This isn't really a creative project," I said now to make her feel better. "Your picture is already traced. All you do is fill it in with colored sand. It's like painting by numbers, only with sand instead of paint."

I was carefully smearing glue on my picture when Lynette and Karen came bouncing over with their completed sand paintings. Karen's looked even worse than Gretchen's flower, but Lynette's horse turned out okay. Of course, I'd rather choke than compliment Miss Goody-goody.

"Ohh, yours is really good," Gretchen said admiringly.

"I'm giving it to my mother for Christmas," Lynette chirped.

"Poor woman," I remarked nastily.

"Kobie," Gretchen said in her that's-not-nice tone. To Lynette, she said, "Kobie's giving hers to her mother, too. Mrs. Roberts is in the hospital, for her back."

"I told you not to step on a crack!" Lynette cried.

"I'm going to step on your face, first chance I get," I said.

"Kobie has a baby-sitter," Gretchen interrupted hastily, to prevent bloodshed.

"She needs one," Lynette sniffed. "But I feel sorry for the baby-sitter, having to watch *her*."

"For your information, I don't have a baby-sitter," I said airily. "Mrs. Blevins is our *housekeeper*. My father hired her to cook and clean and wash clothes and stuff. Nobody baby-sits me. I'm on my own."

"I don't believe it," Lynette scoffed. "You're not old enough."

I sprinkled blue sand on my picture. "A fat lot you know. You probably can't even cross the street by yourself. The truth is," I went on, "I can do exactly as I please. I get to eat what I want, when I want. I can watch anything I want on TV. I can stay up all night. . . ."

Gretchen coughed.

"Well, I *can*," I insisted. "I just haven't felt like it yet. I'll probably stay up tonight, if I'm not too tired. I'm building a secret project, and it's really hard work."

Lynette seemed interested. "What secret project?"

"If I told you, it wouldn't be a secret anymore."

"I still don't believe you, Kobie Roberts,"

Lynette said, clutching her picture. "I bet you're making it all up."

"I really don't care what you believe," I replied haughtily. "I don't have to prove anything to *you*."

When she left, Gretchen said, "Honestly, Kobie, why do you always pick a fight with Lynette?"

"Why does *she* keep bugging me?" I fired back.

"I think she wants to be friends. But you didn't have to tell such a whopper."

I was amazed that my best friend thought I was lying. "If you don't believe me, come on over and I'll show you. Mrs. Blevins waits on me hand and foot. It's great, having a housekeeper. You ought to try it sometime."

"I'll take your word for it, Kobie," Gretchen said. "I never realized you had it so good with Mrs. Blevins."

"Are you kidding? She treats me like a queen." I leaned back in my chair and put my feet up on the table, pretending to be a millionaire. "Ahhhhh. This is the life."

A sharp voice rang out over the buzz of normal classroom conversation. Lynette the Stoolie was pointing at me.

"Mrs. Victor! Kobie's got her feet on the table!"

At first I wasn't sure how I'd like having Mrs. Blevins around.

The Monday after Mrs. Blevins arrived, I woke

up to the wonderful aroma of blueberry pancakes. Mom only fixed pancakes on weekends, but Mrs. Blevins had made pancakes on a Monday morning! I was so hungry, I ran out to the kitchen in my nightgown.

Mrs. Blevins smiled as I skipped over to my place at the table. "Looks like you slept well last night. How many pancakes do you want, Kobie?"

"Four. No, five!"

I ate six pancakes swimming in butter and syrup and three strips of bacon. But I couldn't skip back to my room to get dressed, I discovered. As I dragged my clothes on, I realized why my mother never fixed pancakes on a school morning. I felt like I'd swallowed a battleship.

Mrs. Blevins gave me lunch money, plus extra for ice cream and chocolate milk. She'd convinced Dad that I needed pampering since my mother was in the hospital. I couldn't agree more.

When I got home from school that first day, the house was as spotless as an operating room and smelled delicious. Mrs. Blevins had baked cinnamon rolls topped with gooey vanilla icing for my after-school snack. I scarfed two buns before I even put my books down. Mrs. Blevins was some cook!

"I'm going outside," I informed her after changing into jeans and a sweatshirt. "I have important business, so I'll be back when you see me."

Instead of screaming and yelling like my mother

usually did and demanding that I sign a written document when I'd be back, Mrs. Blevins calmly wrapped three cinnamon rolls in a napkin.

"Take these," she said. "You might get hungry."

I was so astonished that I actually told her what my important business was, the roller coaster ride. She looked impressed.

"I knew the minute I saw you that you were a smart little thing," she acknowledged, adding an orange to my napkin bundle. "What time did you say you'd be back?"

"In about an hour," I replied. "Maybe longer."

Mrs. Blevins couldn't get over my project. "Building a roller coaster! Imagine that! Wait'll I tell my great-grandchildren. They'll want to meet you, Kobie."

Stuffing a cinnamon roll in my mouth, I said, "Well, I don't know if I'll have time. I'm pretty busy. I have a lot of projects going, you know." I might break down and give her great-grandchildren my autograph. For a dollar.

Usually I sprint up the logging road but today I walked. Truthfully, I was now so stuffed I couldn't have run if I'd wanted to. And anyway, since I didn't have to punch a time clock with Mrs. Blevins, I could take my time.

I thought I would get a lot of digging done that day, but I only hacked out a couple of inches of track. The four cinnamon rolls slowed me down so that I could barely lift the pick. But at least I would be able to work on my roller coaster ride every single day, as long as I wanted.

And that's what I did, the next day and the rest of that week. Slowly but steadily, the track was creeping down the road.

On the weekend it rained, and I couldn't work on my roller coaster. Dad was home most of the time, when he wasn't visiting my mother. On Saturday afternoon, he drove Mrs. Blevins to the grocery store. I went, too, and I didn't even have to push the cart. Mrs. Blevins asked me what kind of cereal I wanted and when I couldn't choose, she let me buy both boxes. I also picked out cookies, crackers, candy, and snack cakes. Dad raised his eyebrows when he helped Mrs. Blevins put the groceries away, but he didn't say anything. I guess he bought her suggestion about pampering me with sweets.

By the second week, I was pretty used to having Mrs. Blevins around. She left me alone, when she wasn't fixing me something to eat. If I felt like doing my homework, I did it on the bus. No sweat.

The day we made sand paintings, I took mine home and propped it up on the mantel.

Mrs. Blevins raved over my painting, as if I were the cleverest thing since sliced bread. "You glued colored sand to cardboard and made that pretty picture!" she declared. "Why, you're a real artist, Kobie. I wish my great-grandchildren could see this picture. They just wouldn't believe it!"

"Yeah, but they can't," I said modestly. "I'm giving it to Dad to take to the hospital tomorrow when he visits Mom."

"Won't that be nice?" Mrs. Blevins gushed. "It's a shame you can't give it to her yourself. Poor little thing, separated from your mother like that."

"Oh, it's not so bad," I said bravely. "I'm going out now to work on my roller coaster."

"I packed you some cookies," Mrs. Blevins said, handing me my lightweight jacket. "I put them in your jacket pockets so they'd be easier to carry."

"Thanks," I said, putting it on.

A brisk breeze had blown up since lunch time. The jacket felt good, not too heavy. My mother would have checked the weather forecast and then made me bundle up like an Eskimo. I'd never felt freer in my entire life.

Up on the hill, I hefted the pick with all my might. If I worked really hard the rest of the week, I'd finish the roller coaster! Maybe Gretchen and I could take a trial run that weekend.

I chipped at the roadbed, shivering a little. It was even windier on the hill. The jacket really wasn't heavy enough. Mrs. Blevins should have known I wouldn't be warm enough in it. No, I corrected myself, it wasn't her job. She'd been hired to cook and clean, not to tell me what to do.

The sun was going down. It was getting dark earlier now. Was it supper time yet? Mrs. Blevins wouldn't dare call me. She wasn't supposed to bother me. That was the best part about being independent, I decided. Nobody nagged me about dumb things like supper and homework.

But after a few more futile jabs, I dropped the pick. Although I hadn't dug as far as I intended, I felt tired and empty. I felt the way I had when I let the baby rabbit go free. For some strange reason, the roller coaster ride didn't seem so important anymore.

# 6

"What on earth are you wearing?" Gretchen asked one morning as I sat down at my desk.

"What, this?" I indicated my necklace, a shellacked peanut shell with a painted face and dangling arms and legs. "You've seen my Mr. Peanut necklace before," I said, deliberately misunderstanding her.

"No, I mean on your *feet*." She said it so loud, Lynette O'Bannon and some other kids turned around in their seats.

"Oh, you mean, *this*?" I answered, super-casual. With half the class looking, I stuck my feet out in the aisle so they could observe my outfit better.

Today I wore a sneaker on my left foot and a regular shoe on my right foot. My knee socks didn't match either — I had on a bright green sock and a red sock printed with Scottie dogs.

"Kobie, why are you wearing two different shoes?" Gretchen wanted to know, puzzled. "And two different socks. Did you dress in the dark?"

I waggled my feet like seal flippers. "I'm tired of wearing things that match, that's all. Now that I'm on my own, I can wear what I want."

"You look dumb," Lynette declared.

"You're just jealous," I said, twirling my Mr. Peanut necklace. "You have to wear regular clothes because you mother makes you. *I* don't have to."

"I bet you snuck out of the house before your baby-sitter saw you."

I swung my legs, my red and green socks flashing like a traffic light. "How many times do I have to tell you? Mrs. Blevins is not my baby-sitter. She's the housekeeper. All she does is cook and clean. She doesn't tell me what to do. If I want to wear my bathrobe to school, she can't say anything."

Actually, Mrs. Blevins did give me a funny look when I came out to breakfast and asked, "Are you sure that's what you want to wear to school, Kobie?"

Gretchen giggled at the image of me wearing my flannel bathrobe in the classroom.

"It's true," I said. "Mrs. Blevins lets me do whatever I please. Like this morning. She asked me what I wanted for breakfast, and I said a strawberry milkshake. So she made me one." I sensed my listeners starting to drift into disbelief, so I added hastily, "I had vanilla wafers dipped in peanut butter, too. That's what I wanted for breakfast and that's what I got."

But not without eating a good-for-me breakfast first. Mrs. Blevins wouldn't fix the milkshake until after I had eaten an egg and a piece of toast.

"Bleecchh!" Lynette made a face. "Vanilla wafers and peanut butter, for *breakfast?*"

"You don't know what's good." I pretended to lose interest in the subject.

"But, Kobie," Gretchen said. "That doesn't explain why you wore two different shoes to school."

"I did it because I *wanted* to, Gretch. Don't you ever get tired of wearing the same old thing, like shoes that match?" Pippi Longstocking wore two different-colored socks. She also wore great big shoes so she would have something to grow into, and a dress covered with patches. Pippi didn't bother with proper clothes.

"I think you just have to be different."

"No, I'm just me." But I looked around for Mrs. Victor so she could praise my outfit. *Class,* she'd say, *Kobie makes all her own decisions. Today she decided to be bright and different.* "Where's the teacher?"

"I don't know. It's been five whole minutes since the late bell."

"Maybe she's sick today." As much as I liked Mrs. Victor, having no teacher at all would be even better.

66

"She's here. I saw her," Gretchen said. "Mrs. Warren called her down to the office just before you came. She looked pale and scared. Mrs. Warren, I mean, not our teacher."

I wondered what the school secretary wanted with our teacher. "Maybe Mrs. Victor is in trouble. Old Mr. Leon called to see her."

Gretchen tugged nervously at her ponytail. "I wish she'd come back. It's so noisy in here, somebody's going to yell at us."

The class was getting pretty rowdy. Vincent Wheatly and Richard Supinger were horsing around the terrarium. Bobby Sargent flicked a paper football to Denver Rydell. Even goody-goody Lynette was out of her seat, gossiping with Karen Heinz. With the teacher out of the room, the laughter and chattering got louder and louder.

A furious rapping suddenly silenced all conversation. Mr. Breg stood by Mrs. Victor's desk with a yardstick. He looked angrier than I had ever seen him.

"Stop this commotion right this second," he commanded, rather unnecessarily since everyone had frozen like statues. "Is this the way you behave when your teacher is out of the room? I'm sure she'd be disappointed if she walked in now."

"Where *is* Mrs. Victor?" Lynette asked, slipping into her seat. "She was here but then she left."

"Mrs. Victor is needed in the office," Mr. Breg

replied. "She may not be back for quite some time. Meanwhile, I'm sure she expects you to conduct yourselves as if she were here. Begin your first lesson, *quietly*. If you can't find any work to do, then I will bring over some worksheets to keep you busy."

"No, no, we've got science," Vincent said quickly. Mr. Breg's worksheets were a fate worse than death, at least fifty pages long and packed with tough questions.

We all opened our science books. Mr. Breg nodded. "That's better. I'll be looking in on you from time to time. If I don't find you working, your teacher will hear about it."

As soon as he left to go back across the hall to his own room, a buzz of conversation rose like bees in a clover field.

"Why is Mrs. Victor needed in the office?" I asked Gretchen. "I wonder what's happened?"

Lynette O'Bannon left her seat and went to the blackboard. "You heard what Mr. Breg said. If he hears us talking, he'll give us work. I'm going to take names." Taking a piece of chalk, Lynette numbered one through ten on the blackboard. Her numbers were jiggly and puny, not like Mrs. Victor's bold writing. But her face was plenty determined.

I stood up, too. "Sit down, Lynette. Nobody died and left you king."

She wrote my name beside number one. "You better be quiet, Kobie," she warned. "Or I'll write your name again."

"You spelled it wrong," I said, just to rattle her. When she checked the board, I laughed. "Ha, ha, made you look."

Her mouth set in a thin line, Lynette wrote my name beside number two. Then she plopped herself in Mrs. Victor's chair, arms folded. I decided Lynette would make a great principal one day.

"You can't take anybody's name more than once," I told her.

"If you don't be quiet, Kobie Roberts, I'll write your name all over the board."

Vincent Wheatly shoved his science book aside. "Shut up, both of you. The thing is, where is Mrs. Victor? Is she coming back today or what?"

"What do you care?" I threw at him. "You never do any work anyway."

"Neither do you. All you ever do is draw pictures," Vincent retorted.

Lynette got up and wrote Vincent's name beside number three and my name beside number four.

I couldn't bear the thought of a whole morning being guarded by Lynette and Mr. Breg. Mrs. Victor *was* better than no teacher at all.

"I'm going down to the office," I declared. "I'll ask Mrs. Victor myself when she's coming back." I went up to Mrs. Victor's desk, jerked the center drawer open and took out the wooden hall pass.

"You can't do that!" Lynette shouted, scribbling furiously on the blackboard.

"Watch me." I strode purposefully to the door, which wasn't easy wearing two different kinds of shoes, then marched down the hall. Well, march wasn't exactly the word to describe my uneven bump-clump walk. There's something to be said about wearing shoes that match, I learned. The heel of my tennis shoe was so much flatter than my regular shoe, I had to walk listing to one side like the Leaning Tower of Pisa.

A knot of people had gathered outside the main office. I recognized Mrs. Settinger, the head cafeteria lady, Mr. Burke, the janitor, Mrs. Sharp, the librarian, and the two first-grade teachers whose classes were right next to the office. Through the window I could see Mrs. Warren, the school secretary, slumped on the visitor's sofa with her head in her hands.

The grown-ups spoke in low, serious tones. Nobody noticed me limp past them. Mrs. Warren didn't even look up. I think she was crying.

I found Mrs. Victor in Mr. Leon's office, hanging up the phone.

"Kobie," she said, surprised. "What are you doing out of class?"

"We want to know when you're coming back. Lynette is taking names. She wrote mine down five times already." Shifting my multicolored legs so Mrs. Victor would see them, I glanced around at the principal's office. "Where's Mr. Leon?"

"Your principal had a heart attack this morning," Mrs. Victor replied gravely. "He was rushed to the hospital a little while ago."

"Really?" This shocking news made me forget about impressing Mrs. Victor with my Pippi Longstocking outfit. "He had a heart attack right here in the *school*? We didn't hear any sirens."

"The paramedics didn't turn the sirens on until they were on Lee Highway. We didn't want to upset the children," Mrs. Victor said confidentially, as if I were a grown-up and not one of the children who would cry or shriek at the sound of a siren. "I've been asked to take Mr. Leon's place," she went on. "Your substitute should be here any time."

Substitute! The day brightened instantly. A substitute was almost as good as not having any teacher at all. Everyone knew substitutes were usually pushovers.

"Scoot back to class now, Kobie," Mrs. Victor said. "I have a lot of work to do."

I hobbled to the door. "Mrs. Victor, will Mr. Leon be all right?"

Her eyes were filled with concern. "I certainly hope so, Kobie. We're all hoping he'll recover."

I hurried back to Room 8, anxious to be the first to spread the news. Everyone was talking, though not very loud. Lynette was taking down names as fast as she could write. The blackboard was covered with her thin, loopy printing.

"Guess what?" I announced dramatically. "The principal had a heart attack! Right here in school! The ambulance just took him to the hospital."

Immediately the class erupted with a combination of cheers and questions. The cheers came from Vincent and Richard, both of whom had spent a lot of time in Mr. Leon's office. Even though Mr. Leon wasn't anyone's favorite person, everybody wanted to know more.

"I was right in his office," I said importantly. "I know exactly how it happened. It happened like this."

Sitting in Mrs. Victor's chair, I picked up a pencil and pretended to write a memo. I frowned like Mr. Leon always did, bringing my eyebrows down so low I could barely see. A couple of kids laughed at my impersonation. Suddenly I gasped, clutching my chest as if in terrible pain. I staggered to my feet, only to collapse facedown on the desk. Baring my teeth, I struggled up again and reeled against the blackboard. The entire class seemed spellbound by my performance. Nobody made a sound, not even Lynette.

I decided to drag the "heart attack" out a little longer. From the blackboard I swooned over the world globe, then stumbled toward the wardrobe. Instead of crashing into the wooden doors, I stum-

bled against something cushiony and soft, like
a . . .

My eyes snapped open.

I nearly had a real heart attack.

A strange woman in a blue coat stood stiffly by
the wardrobe, like a tree. She carried a briefcase.
She was not smiling.

"Wh-who are you?" I stammered.

"My name is Miss Price," she replied in a busi-
nesslike tone. "I'm your new teacher. May I ask
what you were doing, young lady?"

She frowned at my mismatched shoes and
socks. I felt more foolish than original. I felt even
dumber having her catch me acting out Mr. Leon's
heart attack.

"Well?" she boomed. "I asked you a question."

"I was just . . . showing the class how Mr. Leon
got sick," I mumbled.

"Your principal is in serious condition," Miss
Price stated. "A heart attack is no laughing matter. I never want to witness such a demonstration
again, is that clear?" I nodded, gulping. "You may
return to your seat."

I slunk back to my chair. Gretchen's eyes were
round. She couldn't believe I'd been caught making fun of the principal, either. I wondered if Miss
Price would send a note home. My mother would
be furious if she found out.

Then a funny thought struck me. This happened

a lot. Whenever I was in the absolute worst trouble, something would seem funny. I could be scared to death and still laugh.

"At least she can't send me to the principal," I whispered to Gretchen, muffling a giggle. But trying not to laugh was worse than laughing. Even though I crammed my fist in my mouth, a huge laugh burst through anyway. The sound rolled around the silent classroom like thunder.

Miss Price glowered at me. "I don't even have my coat off, and you've disrupted this class twice already. What's your name?"

"Kobie," I wheezed. "Kobie Roberts."

"Well, Kobie, would you like to tell us what's so funny? Share your joke with the rest of the class."

"I don't think they want to hear it," I said lamely. "It wasn't very funny." Where did I get the idea that substitutes were pushovers?

She wasn't about to let me off the hook. "Tell us. Stand up and tell us your joke."

Shakily I stood beside my desk. "I just told Gretchen that at least you can't send me to the principal. Because he isn't there, you know."

"Ah, but you're wrong," Miss Price corrected. "You have a new principal. Mrs. Victor."

"Our teacher? But that's just for today," Richard Supinger said doubtfully. "Isn't it?"

Miss Price began unpacking her briefcase with the air of someone who planned to stay a long time. "Mr. Leon will be out many weeks. A person doesn't recuperate from a heart attack in a day or so. Mrs. Victor is taking his place until he returns."

Vincent spoke up. "Isn't Mrs. Victor coming back to teach us anymore?"

"I'm your teacher now," Mrs. Price said firmly. "I don't know what went on in this classroom before I arrived today, but you'll find things will be different. I don't put up with any nonsense." She looked directly at me.

Suddenly self-conscious, I tucked my feet under my desk. I had a feeling Miss Price wouldn't be impressed with a kid who came to school wearing one tennis shoe and one regular shoe.

Only regular shoes would pass muster in Miss Price's class. Or combat boots.

# 7

I was wrong about Miss Price. After she took over as our new teacher, school wasn't like the army.

It was like prison.

Miss Price did everything by the book, just like Mr. Breg. We were going to have spelling tests on Friday, just like Room 9 across the hall. We'd probably even have the same words. And Miss Price handed out a worksheet every five seconds. I hoped the mimeograph machine would blow a gasket, but no such luck.

Worst of all, Miss Price wouldn't let us make our own decisions anymore. Mrs. Victor believed we were responsible citizens. Miss Price treated us like juvenile delinquents one minute, and kindergartners the next. She'd demand absolute silence in the classroom (cell block), and then she'd tell us to line up for recess, two by two, like the little kids. But mostly she acted like she was the warden, and we were her prisoners.

"Time for lock-up," I said glumly one morning as Gretchen and I trudged into class.

She adjusted her yellow ponytail clip. "Oh, Kobie. You exaggerate. Miss Price is different, that's all."

"I'm surprised she doesn't clap us in leg irons. I wish Mrs. Victor would come back," I said. I had yet to find out just *how* different our new teacher was from our old one.

After calling the roll, Miss Price told us to get ready for music. I don't know what we were supposed to get ready for, unless we were supposed to think musical thoughts. Our door was open, and I could hear Room 9 going through the same drill. The sad strains of "On Top of Old Smoky" floated across the hall, made even sadder by the way Mr. Breg's class played.

First Miss Price handed out the instruments. She did this with her usual cheerless manner, as if doling out handcuffs. "Who wants the wooden blocks? Who wants the triangle? Who wants the spoons?" she droned, giving the blocks and triangles and spoons to the few kids who listlessly raised their hands.

The tambourine and the xylophone went to — who else? — the class goody-goodies, Lynette O'Bannon and Karen Heinz. I didn't care. I planned to go to the library anyway.

Then Miss Price went to the board and wrote

77

something, but I couldn't see what. Since she had rearranged the desks into long, jail-cell rows and assigned me the very last seat, I was too far back to see anything. At least Gretchen was still next to me. And Lynette was still in front of me, plus about twelve other kids, all of them seven feet tall.

I stood up to see what the teacher was writing. Miss Price, who apparently had eyes in the back of her head, twirled around.

"Kobie, why are you out of your seat?"

"I'm trying to see what's on the board." I needn't have bothered — all she had written was the name of the song the class was going to murder, "Down by the Old Mill Stream."

"If you can't see, you should have said something. You can trade seats with somebody up here."

Vincent nearly dislocated his arm volunteering. "How about me, Miss Price?" he offered eagerly. "I'll move to the back. I don't mind." I don't suppose he did. Vincent hated sitting at the head of the row. The teacher moved both him and Richard to the front so she could keep an eye on them.

I sat down quickly. "No, no. I can see fine. Lynette's head was in the way for a second."

Lynette half-twisted to frown at me. "My head is not in the way."

"It is, too. It's so fat, nobody can see around it."

"I'm telling Miss Price!"

"Oh, be quiet." I stacked my notebook and library book on my desk. "Gretchen, we're leaving."

Miss Price passed out a mimeographed song sheet. When she gave one to me, I said, "I don't need this. Neither does Gretchen. We're going to the library instead."

"Instead of what?" Miss Price's face was immobile, like a granite wall.

"Music," I answered. "Mrs. Victor always gives us a choice. We can either do music or go to the library. Gretchen and I don't like music, so we go to the library. Will you write us out a pass?" After a few stony seconds, I added, "Please?"

"How can you learn music if you are in the library?" Miss Price asked.

"But Mrs. Victor gives us a *choice!*" Out of the corner of my eye, I could see Gretchen shaking her head, warning me not to argue with the teacher. Maybe Gretchen didn't mind listening to a bunch of kids mutilate "Down by the Old Mill Stream," but *I* did.

"Kobie," Miss Price said. "How many times do I have to tell you that this is no longer Mrs. Victor's class. It's my class. The only choice you have regarding music is if you want to get a good grade or take a zero." She slapped a ditto on my desk.

"I don't have anything to *play*," I pointed out sullenly. "Neither does Gretchen."

79

"You'll have a turn," Miss Price said. "Next time, raise your hand."

For a measly triangle? She must be kidding.

I put my books away, along with the song sheet. I'd sit through stupid old music, but I wouldn't join in. Miss Price would see you can lead a horse to water but you can't make it drink.


"I wonder if we can sue the school for giving us such a crummy teacher," I complained later at lunch.

"I like her," Gretchen said. Miss Price was obviously her kind of a teacher.

"She has mean lips. Did you notice? Like this." I thinned my own lips into a hateful line.

"Kobie, Miss Price has perfectly normal lips."

I shook my head. "You can't trust a teacher with mean lips."

"You might as well pick a state," Gretchen urged. "We have to."

I rolled a hunk of my bread into a doughy little pill. Even though Mrs. Blevins had fixed me exactly what I wanted for lunch — a peanut butter, Fritos, and marshmallow sandwich — I wasn't very hungry. After music, Miss Price had informed the class that we would have to learn all fifty states and their capitals. Even worse, we were supposed to choose a state and write a report.

"Fifty states," I grumbled, squishing another bread pill. "And *fifty* capitals. That's too much for anybody to remember. Who cares what the capital of Montana is, anyway? I'm never going there."

Gretchen smoothed the map she kept in her Nifty notebook. "I knew this would come in handy. You know what worries me?"

"That you won't get your favorite state?" I said sourly. Gretchen couldn't wait to start on her report. She was probably the only kid in class, next to Lynette, who didn't mind Miss Price bossing us every minute of the day. Gretchen never liked making decisions.

"No, silly," she said. "There are fifty states but only twenty-eight kids in our class. Some of us are going to have to do two states, I bet."

I groaned. I hadn't thought of that, but I could guess who would be one of the lucky students to write a report on two states.

"You're right. I'd better pick a state. Let me see that map." Angling her notebook toward me, I scanned the map. None of the states looked very interesting. Florida was a neat shape, though. "Florida, I guess. At least it has alligators."

Gretchen studied the map. "I think I'd like California. Miss Price said she'd have the sign-up sheet ready when we got back from lunch. The test is in three weeks. Our reports are due then, too."

I had heard all this once and didn't care to hear it again. "I hate Miss Price," I commented bitterly.

Gretchen looked shocked. "Kobie, you don't mean that!"

"Yes, I do. School wasn't too bad until she took over. Now I hate school. I hate Mr. Leon for having a heart attack. And I hate Mrs. Victor because she had to take his place." Then I thought of something else. "I bet we won't get to do the fairy tale theater this year."

Mrs. Victor's fifth grade traditionally put on a special program for the primary grades. Years ago, Mrs. Victor had this special theater box built. It had two dowels at the top and bottom and a window covered with a velvet curtain. The best artists in the class would illustrate a fairy tale on a long roll of paper. The story would be wound on the dowels like a scroll, so that a scene at a time appeared in the window. The artists got to wheel the theater around to the lower grades and put on a show. One person would read the story to the class, while the other cranked the scroll.

It was a great honor to work on the project. And it was a lot of fun, too, which automatically ruled out the fairy tale theater from Miss Price's book. Anything that even hinted of fun, she avoided like the plague.

I put my head down. I didn't feel so hot all of a sudden. My stomach hurt. Maybe it was the peanut butter, Fritos, and marshmallow sandwich, but I didn't think so. I think my stomach hurt because Miss Price was making us learn fifty states and fifty capitals. That was enough to upset anyone's stomach.

Sure enough, Miss Price had the sign-up sheet taped to the blackboard when our class got back to Room 8. I saw it before anybody.

"First!" I bellowed, pushing my way up to the blackboard. "Gretchen's second!" I looked around for my friend. She was behind Vincent and Richard, who blocked the line just for meanness.

"Gretchen!" I called. "Up here! I'm saving you a place."

She shook her head helplessly. Gretchen wasn't the type to cut in line, even after being given backsies. Sighing, I scrawled my name in the space beside "Florida," then went and sat down, wondering if I should have claimed the District of Columbia instead.

Gretchen was practically the last person to sign the sheet. When she returned to her desk, she looked unhappy.

"You didn't get California," I guessed.

"Lynette took it," she replied dismally. "By the time I got up there, only the double state reports were left. Kobie, I have to do a report on North *and* South Dakota!"

"You should have cut in line behind me, like I told you to."

"I don't like cutting in line, you know that. I

hate it when somebody butts in front of me." Gretchen closed her Nifty notebook with a magnetic snap.

I didn't tell her that people who cut in line don't end up doing reports on North and South Dakota. No point in rubbing it in.

Miss Price handed out a mimeographed map of the United States, blurrily outlined in lavender. The ditto machine was running out of ink. We were supposed to look up the capitals and fill them in ourselves.

The rest of the afternoon the only sounds in the class were the swish of geography book pages and long, drawn-out sighs. Even Lynette O'Bannon, who normally adored research assignments, restlessly twiddled her pencil between looking up capitals. Life was grim in Miss Price's class. Nobody enjoyed fifth grade any more, least of all me.

When the last bell rang, I slammed my geography book shut and ran out of the room without saying good-bye to Miss Price. I always said good-bye to Mrs. Victor, but the warden didn't deserve the courtesy.

Gretchen and I took different buses this year. Her bus was parked by the curb, but mine hadn't arrived yet.

I waited just inside the front door with the other kids who rode my bus. Mrs. Victor came out of the main office. She smiled when she saw me.

"How are you getting along, Kobie?" she asked.

I shrugged. "Okay."

"I understand your mother has been in the hospital for three weeks now. Is she feeling better?"

"I don't know. She's still in traction. She can't get out of bed." I hadn't seen my mother since the Sunday she left to go to the hospital. I talked to her on the phone every day, though.

Mrs. Victor patted my shoulder. "She'll be home soon. These days are rough, but we'll get through them somehow, won't we?"

It was my turn to ask a question. "How is Mr. Leon? When is he coming back to be our principal?"

"He's doing much better. I think he'll be out of the special heart-patient wing at the end of the week," she replied.

"Then he'll be back in school next week maybe? And you can be our teacher again?" I asked hopefully.

Mrs. Victor shook her head. "No, dear, I'm afraid Mr. Leon isn't coming back this year. He's had a very serious illness."

"Not coming back! Then — " I swallowed as a new, terrible thought dawned. "You won't ever be our teacher again, will you?"

"I'm sorry, Kobie," she said gently.

Tears sprang into my eyes. I blinked them back. "And we have to have the war — Miss Price the rest of the year? Can't we get another substitute?"

"Miss Price is a very fine teacher, Kobie. She

told me just yesterday how much she enjoys the class."

I found that hard to swallow. "She doesn't like any of us, Mrs. Victor. She just said that. She's mean and she doesn't let us make our own decisions like you did. I don't like her."

"Kobie," Mrs. Victor said. "Miss Price has her way of teaching, just as I have my way of teaching. We're different people, so our teaching methods are bound to be different. Give her a chance." She glanced in the direction of the loading zone. "You bus is here, Kobie. I'll see you tomorrow. Remember, chin up."

I sat by myself on the ride home, gloomily staring out the window with my chin down, not up. I kept thinking about what Mrs. Victor had said, about Mr. Leon never coming back. One morning he was our principal, and then suddenly he wasn't. He went into the hospital, and now he wasn't coming back to school, not ever.

Which meant our class was stuck with Miss Price for the rest of fifth grade. In my mind's eye, I saw miles of mimeographed worksheets, stretched out like an endless purple road.

Then I remembered the day Lynette had taunted me with that babyish rhyme, "Step on a crack, break your mother's back, step on a line, break your mother's spine." I had stomped on every single crack, deliberately, and suddenly my mother had gone to the hospital. Suppose my mother wasn't coming back, either?

When I walked into the house, I was surprised to find Mrs. Blevins sitting in the living room. She was peeling potatoes while watching a soap opera. My mother *never* peeled potatoes in the living room in her entire life. She didn't watch soap operas, either.

But what really got me was the way Mrs. Blevins sat, with her feet planted firmly on the rug. She looked . . . permanent. As if she intended to stay forever.

"Hello, Kobie," she greeted me warmly. "I've fixed you some nice brownies and milk. You'll want a snack before you go back outside."

Wearily I dropped my books on a chair. "I'm not very hungry."

Potato peelings spiraled neatly from the paring knife. "You ought to have something to eat before you go out to work on your Ferris wheel," she advised.

"Roller coaster. I'm digging a roller coaster track, not a Ferris wheel."

"It's still hard work for a growing girl. You need to keep up your strength."

Would she get off it? "I *said* I'm not hungry. I had a big lunch," I added in a slightly nicer tone. "Anyway, I don't think I'm going to work on my roller coaster ride today."

It was funny, but since I was able to work on my project any time I wanted, I didn't feel like working on it as much.

Mrs. Blevins pushed herself out of the chair. "We're having roast beef and mashed potatoes tonight. Doesn't that sound yummy? But your poor father will be home late again, I'm afraid."

"Is he going to visit Mom on his way home from work?" I hardly ever saw Dad anymore. He left for work before I got up in the morning, and he didn't come home until eight-thirty or nine at night.

"That man will wear himself out, going from work to the hospital every single night," Mrs. Blevins predicted.

"I'll call Mom after supper," I said. Mrs. Blevins nodded approvingly. I talked to my mother every day. If I didn't call her, she called me. Tonight I especially wanted to talk to her. For some reason, I needed to hear her voice.

Instead of watching television, I stayed in my room. From my junk drawer I took a big sheet of construction paper — my last — and lay down on the floor with my colored pencils and stubby crayons. When I was little and the teacher let us draw whatever we wanted, I always drew the same thing. A farm.

While the other kids hurriedly scribbled a house or a cat, I filled the whole piece of paper with detailed little buildings. I started with the farmhouse and surrounded it with a pigsty, a duck pond with ducks on it, a cow barn, a chicken coop . . . things you'd expect to see on a farm. It was comforting, somehow, to create a world that was all mine, even if only on a sheet of crinkly beige paper.

As autumn shadows gathered outside, I drew a rectangular farmhouse, a pigsty with little pigs, a duck pond with ducks on it, a rabbit hutch with bunnies, and so on. Then I colored my drawing, being extra careful not to cross any lines.

# 8

"How many of these things do we have to make?" Gretchen wondered out loud. A bunch of crumpled paper pumpkins lay discarded around her chair.

"I'm only doing one," I replied. I didn't want to brag, but my pumpkin was going to be a master-piece. It would be the best decoration in the cafeteria.

We were supposed to have music today, but because it was the day before Halloween, Miss Price was actually letting us make decorations for the all-school Halloween party tomorrow after-noon. Of course, we had to make exactly what Mr. Breg's class was making — pumpkins and witches cut out of black and orange construction paper. The world would probably end if we did something different from Mr. Breg's class.

But *my* pumpkin was different. Instead of fold-ing orange paper in half and snipping out a half-circle, the way little kids cut out Valentine hearts, I drew a great big huge pumpkin freehand. It took up almost a whole sheet of paper. Then I cut out his eyes, nose, and mouth. The other kids pasted black triangles on to their pumpkins to make the faces, but I had a better idea.

"Look at Lynette's witch chain," Gretchen commented. "Isn't it cute?"

"Yeah." I barely glanced at Lynette's paper chain. "Her witches are kind of lumpy, though."

"I don't think so. Lynette's a good artist."

"As good as me?" I challenged.

"Nobody is as good as you, Kobie," my best friend admitted loyally, cutting another pumpkin from construction paper. She laid five pumpkins in a row and began drawing jack-o'-lantern faces on them. I noticed Gretchen didn't even try to make the expressions different. All her pumpkins looked the same, like they'd been stamped from a factory.

"What are you wearing tomorrow night?" she asked.

"Last year's witch costume. It still fits, so I guess I'll wear it again this year." I concentrated on folding the flaps of a triangular-shaped box made out of black constuction paper. My idea was harder to do than I thought. But I was determined to make it work.

"I'll be a gypsy again," Gretchen said. "Are you going trick-or-treating with your cousins?"

"Sure. I go with them every year."

Since we lived on Lee Highway, where there

were very few houses, my parents drove me to the next town so I could go around with my cousins. Gretchen lived in Willow Springs, too, but her house was on a back road with lots of other houses. She went trick-or-treating in her own neighborhood. One year I went around with Gretchen. It was fun, but I really looked forward to getting together with my cousins. We'd gather a big gang and prowl the streets for hours.

Talking about trick-or-treating and my witch costume was putting me in a scary mood. A good kind of scary, though. Halloween was my favorite holiday. I liked it even better than Christmas. As I taped triangular-shaped boxes behind the cut-out eyes, nose, and mouth of my great big pumpkin, I hummed "Down by the Old Mill Stream." I decided to get my witch costume out after school today. Mom kept it in the linen closet, so I could take it out any time I wanted. Sometimes I wore the cape when I was feeling witchy.

"I'm done," Gretchen said, lining up her five identical jack-o'-lanterns.

"Me, too." I held up my oversized pumpkin. "Say hello to Jack."

"Kobie, he looks real!" Gretchen said admiringly.

He did look real. The black paper boxes behind the features made the pumpkin seem three-dimensional. I added brown and gold paper leaves at the bottom, so Jack appeared to be sitting on a pile of oak leaves. He could have been right out of some farmer's field.

Miss Price glided over to our table. "Are you girls finished? What nice pumpkins, Gretchen. All alike, too. How neat. And what have you made, Kobie?"

"This." Proudly, I handed her my wonderful jack-o'-lantern.

"Oh, he's adorable!" she exclaimed. If I hadn't felt so terrific, I would have fainted. Miss Price hardly ever praised anything I did, much less my artwork.

But her next sentence squashed my terrific feeling.

"Why, he's as cute as Lynette's paper witch chain," she went on inconsiderately. "Did you see it?"

I nodded numbly. Why did Miss Price have to compare my wonderful pumpkin to Lynette's witch chain? Jack was a hundred times better than a bunch of paper dolls.

"What else did you make?" Miss Price asked me.

I stared at her. "Nothing. It took me all this time to make Jack."

She nudged paper scraps with the toe of her shoe. "You used quite a lot of paper. I just thought you made more decorations. Gretchen made five."

Now I was fuming. My pumpkin was a masterpiece! A person only made *one* masterpiece at a time. Surely she didn't expect me to cut out a zillion Jacks the way Gretchen cut out her plain old pumpkins? Or a whole chain of Jacks like Lynette's dumb witch chain?

Mrs. Victor wouldn't have expected me to crank out a dozen decorations for the Halloween party. She would have complimented everybody, no matter how many or few decorations each student made. But she would have complimented me a teeny bit *more*. Not a whole lot more. Just enough to let me know mine was really special.

Miss Price didn't know anything about making true artists feel special. She'd probably stick my wonderful pumpkin on the ice cream freezer or some other dumb place, where nobody would see it.

As soon as I got home from school, I went to the linen closet and took out the box that contained my Halloween costume. I lifted the lid with shivery excitement. Halloween was tomorrow, and I was going to be the best witch ever!

On top was the shiny black cape with sparkly gold moons and stars sprinkled all over it. The long black skirt was plain, but the pointed hat glittered with more moons and stars. It was the greatest costume in the world. I hoped I would never outgrow it.

I put the cape on, tying the strings around my neck. I felt witchy already!

I swished into the kitchen on an imaginary broom, my cape whipping behind me.

"Whoo!" Mrs. Blevins cried, almost dropping a pan of corn bread. "A witch in the house!"

"It's just me," I said, jumping into my chair.

"Well, you scared the life out of me!" Mrs. Blevins exclaimed.

"Tomorrow night is Halloween," I informed her, in case she hadn't looked at a calendar in the past year. "We're having a party at school, and then I'm going trick-or-treating with my cousins. I can't wait!"

"Sounds like fun. I think I'll make some candied apples for the little hobgoblins."

"Oh, we never have trick-or-treaters," I said. "There aren't any other kids around here but me. That's why I go to Manassas. Only old people live around here, and they don't know anything about Halloween."

"Is that right?" Mrs. Blevins' dimples winked with amusement.

The back door opened and my father came in, carrying his lunch box.

"Dad, you're early!" I leaped up to hug him. "Will you be early tomorrow, too? I'm supposed to go trick-or-treating with my cousins, remember?"

Dad rubbed his forehead. He seemed tired. "Kobie, I'm sorry, but I can't take you to Manassas tomorrow night. I have to work late. By

95

the time I get through visiting your mother, it'll be after eleven when I come home."

"You have to take me!" I shrieked. "It's Halloween! And I want to go trick-or-treating!"

"I'm sorry," he repeated. "I know it means a lot to you, but you'll have to accept it, Kobie. Things are different this year, with your mother in the hospital."

"What if you don't visit her one night?" I said desperately. "What if you came straight home from work and took me? Mom would understand."

He shook his head. "I won't quit work until nine-thirty. By the time we drive to Manassas, it'd be after ten. That's still too late for you to be out."

"No, it isn't!" I protested. "Only the real little kids go trick-or-treating early anyhow. It'll be good and spooky by then."

"Kobie, you know as well as I do, you can't roam the streets of Manassas that late." He put his lunch box on the counter with a weary clunk. "I'm very sorry. I can't do anything about it, though. I have to work."

"I'll have to wait a whole year before I can go trick-or-treating again!" I stormed. "My Halloween is ruined!"

"Kobie, dear," Mrs. Blevins said consolingly. "What about the nice party you're having at school tomorrow? That'll be lots of fun."

"No, it won't," I said, close to tears. "School

96

parties are dumb. I don't want any supper." With that, I ran to my room.

Mrs. Blevins must have started after me, because I heard my father say, "Let her go. She needs to cry it out. I think she misses her mother more than she lets on."

He was wrong, wrong, wrong! I wasn't missing my mother — well, no more than usual. I was going to miss *Halloween*. Parents think they know everything. But they don't know anything about kids. Especially their own kids.

The next day I pretended I couldn't care less about Halloween. Everybody was excited, and it wasn't easy to be, since Mr. Breg and Miss Price made us slave the whole day until it was time for the party.

We lined up by class and trooped down to the cafeteria. At the doors, we had to wait before we could go inside.

"Isn't this neat?" Gretchen chirped. "I just love school parties." She was in a bubbly mood, but then nobody had yanked Halloween out from under *her*.

I yawned to show the whole thing bored me to death. "At least we get out of arithmetic. I'm surprised the warden doesn't work it into the party somehow. Make us count cupcakes and divide by the cookies or something."

"Kobie, you never have anything nice to say about Miss Price," Gretchen said. "She really isn't that bad."

"She's terrible." But then, any teacher would have been terrible, coming after Mrs. Victor.

The doors opened and we filed into the cafeteria.

Lynette squealed, "Look! You'd never know it was the cafeteria, the way it's all decorated."

"Yeah," I said sarcastically. "I never would have recognized the milk cooler or the tables and chairs or the trash cans. What a transformation."

"Oh, you're just an old grouch." Lynette went off to find Karen Heinz.

"The food is over here." I pulled Gretchen toward the tables under the windows. "If we hurry, we'll get the best stuff."

The room mothers must have worked overtime. Dozens of platters of frosted cupcakes and special Halloween cookies covered the tables. Miss Dede, a first-grade teacher, ladled "Witch's Brew" into paper cups. I snatched one and drank it in one gulp.

"Hawaiian punch with ginger ale," I pronounced, filching two more cups, one for Gretchen and a second for me.

By pushing only a couple of little kids, I managed to get four of the best cupcakes: chocolate, with thick orange icing studded with candy corn.

Gretchen and I found a quiet corner where we

could eat. Lynette and Karen drifted over, sipping "Witch's Brew" from punch cups.

"What time are you guys going trick-or-treating?" Karen asked us.

"I'm not going," I replied breezily.

"Not going!" Gretchen said. "I thought you were supposed to go with your cousins."

Casually I picked the candy corn off my second cupcake. "I don't want to go this year. Trick-or-treating is for babies."

"I'm going," Lynette said.

"So'm I," Karen chimed.

I buffed my fingernails on my sleeve. "I rest my case."

Gretchen didn't say anything. I knew she was going trick-or-treating, too. She probably thought I included her in my insult. I felt bad, but I didn't want anybody to know I couldn't go trick-or-treating because my father had to work late. After all, everybody was convinced I was totally independent.

"Did you see where they hung my witch chain?" Lynette boasted.

I stuffed pleated cupcake wrappers into my empty cup. "On the garbage cans?"

"No, that's where they put *your* decoration," she laughed. "My chain is hanging over the door. Everybody loves it."

My eyes flew to the corner where kids threw

trash away and stacked dirty trays. Sure enough, my fabulous pumpkin was taped to the wall above the trash cans! I couldn't believe it! Miss Price probably did it on purpose, to tell me what she thought of me and my artwork.

At that moment, the Warden herself strolled over. "Having a good time, girls?" Miss Price asked.

"Who put my pumpkin over by the garbage cans?" I demanded.

Miss Price glanced in the direction I was indignantly pointing. "I guess one of the sixth-graders. They were responsible for hanging the decorations."

I was outraged. Teachers were supposed to make sure their best students' artwork was displayed in a place of *honor* — not hanging over the garbage cans. "I want it down, right now. It doesn't belong there! Doesn't anybody care about fine art around here?"

"I don't like your tone, young lady," Miss Price said sternly. "Since you're obviously not enjoying yourself, I think you ought to go back upstairs until the buses come."

With everyone staring at me, I stamped over and jerked my pumpkin down. I tossed it into the trash can, then flounced out of the cafeteria.

There wasn't a living soul in the halls or in the classrooms. In my classroom, I sat at my desk, steaming. When my anger cooled down, I realized how strange it felt to be sitting there with the room completely deserted. Everybody in the entire school was downstairs having a blast.

"Kobie." A familiar voice broke the silence. Mrs. Victor walked into the room. "I was just on my way to the party. Why aren't you there?" Mr. Leon, the old principal, never went to all-school parties. It occurred to me that Mrs. Victor was a lot better principal than Mr. Leon had been.

"Miss Price sent me back, but I wanted to come back anyway." I tried to look as though it was more my idea than a punishment.

"Why?"

"Somebody put my decoration over the garbage cans, and I told her I didn't like it. I didn't really want to go to the party. You're not missing anything."

Mrs. Victor leaned against Lynette's desk. "Kobie, I know you're having a hard time with your mother away. But you shouldn't fight Miss Price. She's on your side."

I didn't believe it. Nobody was on my side, except Gretchen. And maybe not even her anymore, since I insulted her about wanting to go trick-or-treating.

"Give Miss Price a chance," Mrs. Victor said on her way out. "Okay?"

Why should I? Miss Price hadn't given *me* a chance yet.

When the last bell rang, I ran down the hall to the buses. For once, my bus was on time. I jumped on, glad I didn't have to face any of the kids from my class.

At home, I went directly to my room. This was supposed to be a fun day, and it had turned out awful. Without changing my school clothes, I crawled in bed. If I was going to miss Halloween, I wanted it to be over fast. Mrs. Blevins knocked on my door once. I told her to go away.

I must have fallen asleep, because it was completely dark when I woke up. Voices murmured outside my door. Mrs. Blevins and Dad, talking about me, undoubtedly. Then my door creaked open and yellow light arrowed across my bed. I squinched my eyes against the glare. Someone tiptoed into my room, making rustling noises. Then the door closed again and I was alone.

I switched on my lamp. To my surprise, I saw a hollow plastic pumpkin on my nightstand, brimming with candy bars and little bags of candy corn. I knew instantly who had sent it.

My mother.

It had to be Mom. Mrs. Blevins didn't drive. And my father had been busy working all day, so it couldn't have been him, either. That left my mother. She was the only one who really understood how much Halloween meant to me.

I picked up the pumpkin by its black plastic strap and tucked it in bed with me. The roundness of the pumpkin felt nice against my stomach and the faint smell of chocolate was comforting. There *was* someone else on my side.

Holding that thought, I fell asleep again.

The next morning, I took my pumpkin out to the breakfast table.

"Where did this come from?" I asked Mrs. Blevins.

She drizzled melted butter over an enormous waffle. "Why, your dear mother sent that home with your father last night. Evidently she had one of the nurses buy the pumpkin in the gift shop. The candy was donated from the patients' supper trays. Everybody heard about the poor little girl who had to miss trick-or-treating."

I watched Mrs. Blevins put away the dishes from my father's breakfast. She knew exactly where everything went, even the waffle iron. Mrs. Blevins acted like our house was hers.

Suddenly I wanted my mother. I was tired of Mrs. Blevins sitting in my mother's chair, saying nice things all the time. I wanted my mother to come home and make me hamburgers just the way I liked them and tuck me in at night with the silly little rhyme.

But *could* Mom come home, with the efficient Mrs. Blevins taking her place? I had begun to think the real reason our principal wasn't coming back to school was because Mrs. Victor was doing such a good job as principal. And as long as Mrs. Blevins was around to fix waffles, even on a weekday morning, my father wouldn't be in any rush to bring my mother home.

It was *my* fault my mother had to go to the hospital in the first place. If I hadn't stepped on all those cracks, my mother's back would be fine.

So it was up to me to help my mother come home to her rightful place.

And the only way to do that, I figured, was to get rid of Mrs. Blevins.

# 9

My brilliant idea came to me on the bus going to school. The perfect plan to get rid of Mrs. Blevins.

Actually, the bus driver gave me the idea at the Wellborns' stop. The Wellborns were the worst kids in Centreville Elementary, loud-mouthed troublemakers who would do anything to get attention. By some miracle, I didn't have a Wellborn in my class, even though there were seven of them.

Mr. Bass slowed the bus to a halt, and the Wellborns boiled on, punching each other and yelling, the way they always did.

"Find seats!" Mr. Bass ordered them. He wasn't allowed to move the bus until everybody was sitting down. The Wellborns always took their sweet time finding seats.

The bus started up again. Mr. Bass muttered, "What holy terrors. I pity their poor teachers."

I happened to be sitting right behind him.

105

Something in his tone made me lean forward. "Mr. Bass, what did you just say?"

He glanced in the rearview mirror, eyebrows quirked. He probably didn't think anybody heard him. "Yes, Kobie?" It was hard to hear on the bus, with the noisy engine and the Wellborns screaming their lungs out.

I hung over the pole that divided the driver's seat from the rest of the bus. "I said, what did you call those kids? Holy something."

He chuckled. "Holy Terrors. That's what they are, all right."

"What does it mean?"

"It means those kids are a real handful. They'd try the patience of a saint. I wonder how their teachers make it through the day." He turned the bus into the loading zone in front of Centreville Elementary.

As I whipped into the aisle to get off first, Mr. Bass said, "Bye, Kobie. Have a nice day."

I smiled at him. "Mr. Bass, I'm going to have a wonderful day!"

I pelted down the hall to my class, even though running in the building was strictly forbidden. I couldn't wait to tell Gretchen about my idea.

She was already at her desk, copying geography notes off the blackboard. She looked a little miffed and then I remembered the party yesterday. Gretchen obviously still thought I believed she was a baby because she went trick-or-treating.

106

Before she could say anything, I blurted, "Gretchen, I'm sorry about what I said yesterday. I was just mad because I couldn't go trick-or-treating last night. I have to make Mrs. Blevins leave so my mother will come home again. I've decided to become a Holy Terror. Will you help me?"

"What?" she exclaimed. "You're going to become a *what?*"

"Holy Terror. That's what Mr. Bass called the Wellborns this morning when they got on the bus. You know how awful they are. Mr. Bass said he didn't know how their teachers put up with them." I paused to take a deep breath. "See, if you're a holy terror, nobody can stand you. That's what I want to be, to get rid of Mrs. Blevins."

"Did she keep you from going trick-or-treating?" Gretchen asked, goggle-eyed.

I shook my head. "My father had to work late, and he couldn't take me. This morning I decided — promise you won't laugh? — I want my mother back home."

"I can understand that," Gretchen said, "but why do you want to make the housekeeper leave? I thought she was perfect, because she lets you do what you want."

"She's too perfect! Gretchen, she fixes waffles for breakfast and keeps the house sterilized. My mother will never be able to come home as long as Mrs. Blevins is there. I think this traction Mom's in is just an excuse to keep her away. Dad will never get rid of Mrs. Blevins. But if I'm awful enough, Mrs. Blevins won't be able to stand me and she'll quit."

Lynette, who had just sat down in front of me, tossed back a remark. "Well, that shouldn't be too hard."

"Mind your own beeswax, O'Bannon." Lowering my voice, I said to Gretchen, "We'll talk some more at lunch. Be thinking of ways I can be awful."

One thing about Gretchen, she pitches in whenever I've got a problem, without asking a million questions. Gretchen got right on the assignment. Taking a piece of paper from her Nifty notebook, she headed it, *Ways Kobie Can Be Awful.*

By lunch time we'd thought up three ways I could be awful. At our table in the cafeteria, I reviewed the list.

*Mess up the house every single day.*
*Tangle her knitting yarn.*
*Hide her glasses.*

"I can tell who thought up the last one," Gretchen said wryly.

I read the list again. "These are pretty good, especially messing up the house. I don't know which to do first."

"Why not all of them?"

I considered that angle. "No. If I mess up the

house and hide her glasses and tangle her knitting all at once, she'll think I've gone crazy. She might call the men in the white coats. I want to drive *her* batty. I think I ought to do it little by little."

"I guess you know more about driving people crazy than anybody." Gretchen pulled four candy bars from her lunch bag. "I brought extra for you, since you said you weren't going trick-or-treating last night."

All around us, kids were trading trick or treat goodies. The day after Halloween was the best day to take lunch. Vincent Wheatly's lunch bag sagged with candy — he didn't even bother with a sandwich.

"Thanks," I said. Even though Gretchen's feelings were hurt, she still brought me candy. She was the greatest. "My mom sent me some stuff from the hospital. Sort of like a Halloween Easter basket."

When I described my goodie pumpkin, Gretchen said, "That was really nice of your mom. No wonder you want her home."

Next to us, Lynette peeled the cellophane off a miniature box of raisins. She tipped her head back and dribbled the raisins into her mouth.

I made a face. "Blecchh! She just ate a whole bunch of squished bugs!"

Gretchen shrieked in disgust. "Stop it, Kobie! I happen to like raisins. You always say terrible things when people are eating."

Suddenly I had a new item to add to the list.

"That's it, Gretch! I'll gross out Mrs. Blevins!" I cried joyfully. "That'll drive her dingbats for sure. And I'm so good at it!" I grinned wickedly at Gretchen's expression of horror. She knew just *how* gross I could be at the table.

Probably because I refused to eat the night before, Mrs. Blevins outdid herself at supper. She made fried chicken, mashed potatoes, cream gravy, peas with little pearl onions, rolls, and lemon meringue pie. We normally had that kind of dinner on Sunday. But this was Thursday. When I saw the table with all that delicious food on it, I knew my mother's chances were slipping by the minute. Another two or three meals like this and my mother could forget about coming home.

For once, Dad was on time. He had visited my mother during his lunch hour, because the school he was working at was near the hospital.

"Ah, what a luxury to come home before dark," he said as we sat down. "And to such a meal! Mrs. Blevins, you shouldn't have gone to so much trouble."

She blushed modestly as she passed the potatoes. "Oh, it wasn't any trouble. Poor Kobie didn't eat a bite last night. I wanted to fix her a special supper."

"Well, it sure is good," Dad said, digging in with relish.

110

I couldn't waste another second. Pushing the pearl onions away from the peas, I commented, "I don't like these slimy little onions. They're like eating eyeballs." Then I put a huge forkful of mashed potatoes and peas in my mouth and chewed with my mouth open wide enough to show my tonsils.

Mrs. Blevins handed me a napkin. "Kobie, dear, we chew with our mouths closed."

Dad frowned at me across the table. "She knows that."

I pulled a chunk of meat off the drumstick Mrs. Blevins laid on my plate and began dissecting it with my knife.

"What are you doing?" Dad asked suspiciously.

"Looking for veins. In science we're learning about blood vessels and stuff, and Miss Price said you could easily find veins in chicken meat. Got one!" I held up a piece of meat with a dark line running through it.

My father stopped gnawing his own drumstick. He drank some water quickly.

"I bet you make straight A's in science," Mrs. Blevins said, obviously trying to change the subject.

"Nah. More like straight C's. A few weeks ago we had to cut up a lima bean. You know, to find the itty bitty lima bean plant?" I rattled innocently on, despite a dirty look from my father. "The plant is inside that fingernail-like part of the lima bean."

"Fingernail-like part?" Mrs. Blevins echoed.

"Yeah. The hard part along the bottom. It's like eating fingernails."

Dad said warningly, "Kobie."

"Where does the child come up with such fanciful notions?" Mrs. Blevins asked him.

"Kobie has strange descriptions for the foods she doesn't like."

He just gave me the perfect opening to do a super gross-out on Mrs. Blevins!

"Want to hear some of them?" I asked brightly, then rushed on before anyone could protest. "Sliced bananas are like eating slugs, whole. It's so yucky the way they slide down. And the pulpy stuff in orange juice is like drinking fish scales, don't you think?"

"I've never thought of orange juice that way," Mrs. Blevins said mildly.

"Grapes remind me of eyeballs, just like these slick little onions. Raisins are worse — they're exactly like squished bugs. And those flecks in pizza remind me of scabs — "

"Kobie!" Dad interrupted angrily. "That's enough! What's gotten into you this evening?"

"Nothing." I pushed my food around my plate, dismayed.

My super gross-out had failed. Mrs. Blevins hadn't turned pale or bolted for the bathroom or anything. She just sat there with a slight smile on her face. She probably didn't care what I said about her food, as long as I ate.

Then I remembered how upset Mrs. Blevins had been yesterday when I didn't eat supper. If I went on a hunger strike, she'd resign for sure! She couldn't stand it when people didn't appreciate her cooking.

"I'm not hungry," I declared in a ringing voice, putting my napkin across my plate.

"I'm hardly surprised," Dad said. "The things you talked about, none of us should be hungry. Eat your supper, Kobie. Mrs. Blevins worked hard to fix this meal. And it's good."

She beamed at me. "I made your favorites tonight."

"I don't like chicken anymore," I said snootily. "Too many blood vessels."

Dad's chair scraped back. "Go to your room, Kobie. If you're not hungry, then the rest of us would like to eat in peace."

I retreated gladly to my room. I needed to think about this hunger strike a little more. Thanks to my mother, I had enough candy to last me several days, if I didn't get greedy. And Gretchen could be counted on to bring me an extra sandwich to school.

Gleefully, I hugged my biggest panda bear. If I refused to eat Mrs. Blevins' cooking, Dad would have to get rid of her! He wouldn't let his own child starve to death.

The next morning, I ignored Mrs. Blevins when she asked me what I wanted for breakfast. And

I left the lunch she fixed me on the counter. In the pocket of my jacket, I smuggled four candy bars, which I gobbled at the bus stop. Gretchen brought two extra peanut butter sandwiches in her lunch. I had more candy for dessert. Hunger strikes weren't so bad.

At supper that night, Mrs. Blevins tried to tempt me with hot dogs and chocolate pudding. I sailed past the kitchen with my nose in the air. After my father came home, I overheard Mrs. Blevins tell him in a worried voice I wasn't eating anything. Of course, I had to hide behind the couch to overhear their conversation, but I needed to find out if my hunger strike was working.

"I don't know what else to do," Mrs. Blevins said, on the verge of despair. "The poor child won't eat a morsel. She'll starve!"

"I expect Kobie's filling up on Halloween candy," came Dad's conclusion.

Mrs. Blevins wasn't reassured. "I'm afraid she'll get weak and catch pneumonia."

"You know, Mrs. Blevins, Kobie has always been a very headstrong child," my father said. "Did you know she ran away once because her mother served pork chops?" Behind the sofa, I squirmed uncomfortably. I hated to be reminded of that embarrassing story.

"Kobie came out to the table, saw a pork chop lying on her plate, and left the house. She walked across the field to the neighbor's house, knocked on the door, and when the woman answered the door, told her she was moving in, but only if they never had pork chops. She was five years old."

Mrs. Blevins clucked her tongue. "I declare. Kobie is a bit of a trial, I must admit."

"I wouldn't worry," Dad advised. "When she gets hungry enough, she'll eat. I expect she's already getting tired of candy three times a day."

Well! Obviously my father didn't care that I might catch pneumonia! But he was right about one thing — I *was* pretty tired of Halloween candy. Hershey bars were great, but not as a steady diet. I wasn't sure how much longer I could hold out.

When Mom called that night, I galloped to the telephone.

"How are you, Kobie? Do you miss me? I miss you." She said that every night. Tonight it was especially nice to hear.

"Mom! I'm trying to get you home," I whispered into the receiver, in case Mrs. Blevins was hanging around.

"What? Kobie, what are you talking about?"

"Don't worry," I told her. "I'll come up with a plan to get you home as soon as possible. They won't replace you. I won't let them!"

When I went to bed, I tried to think of a new plan, but my brain wasn't working right. Probably too many Hershey bars. It was hard to hatch a new scheme when my stomach kept rumbling and my mind kept wandering to the leftover chicken in the refrigerator. I was dying for a drumstick, veins and all.

The next morning I staggered out to the kitchen, weak from hunger. "I don't want any breakfast," I said feebly.

Mrs. Blevins set a tantalizing plate of pancakes in front of me. My mouth watered like a lawn sprinkler. Real food!

"You love pancakes, don't you?" she coaxed. "And you like my cream gravy, so I made you some, special. You need something to stick to your ribs."

Gravy on pancakes? I'd never had that combination before, but it smelled delicious. Actually, I would have eaten old motor oil poured over pot holders, I was so hungry.

I devoured every crumb and then licked the plate down to the flowered design. When there wasn't anything left, I laid down my fork, feeling guilty. What a traitor I was, giving in so easily! My hunger strike had to be the shortest on record, not even a day. If I couldn't drive Mrs. Blevins crazy any better than this, my mother had better order new address labels, with the hospital address on them.

"What would you like for supper?" Mrs. Blevins asked, encouraged by my gleaming plate. "You can have anything you want."

The pancakes and cream gravy were really good. Too bad I couldn't have them every morning. Then it dawned on me that I *could* have pancakes and gravy every morning — Mrs. Blevins would fix me anything I wanted. So . . . why not for supper, too? If I couldn't drive Mrs. Blevins crazy, maybe I could make *Dad* mad enough to fire her!

"I'd like pancakes and gravy tonight," I told her. "They're my new favorite food."

Mrs. Blevins looked delighted. "Whatever you say."

True to her word, Mrs. Blevins made pancakes and gravy for supper. If Dad thought having pancakes for supper was strange, he didn't say so.

I repeated my request at breakfast the next morning and again at supper that evening. Mrs. Blevins asked Dad to stop at the store on his way home and buy more pancake mix.

I had pancakes and gravy for breakfast, and pancakes and gravy for dinner, six days in a row. I could barely *face* a plate of pancakes, which were beginning to taste like fried wool, and the sight of the pancake mix box made me break out in a cold sweat, but I stuck to my resolve. Twice, Dad had to bring home an extra gallon of milk and another box of mix. Mrs. Blevins fried sausage and apples to go with Dad's meals but he ate pancakes and gravy every day, too, because Mrs.

Blevins always made a gallon of pancake batter and gravy. He was so distracted he hardly knew what he was eating anyway.

On the seventh evening, Dad came home late. I could tell he was really beat. He probably wanted a good supper, with meat and vegetables. Something he could chew.

I stationed myself behind the couch and waited for Mrs. Blevins to present him with pancakes and gravy. Surely he'd hit the ceiling and fire her.

"Pancakes," Dad said heavily.

"I'm sorry, Mr. Roberts, I made so much batter and it'd be a shame to waste it," Mrs. Blevins apologized. "This is all the dear child will eat."

"I wish the dear child would get off this pancake kick." Then he added, "These pancakes are even better than the ones you made this morning."

Behind the couch, I clenched my fists in frustration. What was *wrong* with them? They both ought to be nuts by now — Mrs. Blevins because she had to fix pancakes and gravy twice a day, and Dad because he had to eat it. But they weren't budging!

"Kobie's not the easiest child to put up with," Dad said. My own father! "Her mother and I really appreciate your staying here."

"The poor dear motherless lamb," Mrs. Blevins cooed. "I'll stay as long as she needs me."

# 10

Gretchen clumped over to our library table with a stack of *World Book* encyclopedias. "I found a book for you," she said, taking a smaller book off the top of the pile. "It's about Florida."

I looked up from my drawing of an alligator. "Thanks. But I don't need it."

"I wish I could find a whole book about North and South Dakota," Gretchen lamented. "There just aren't any in our school library. Lynette found two books about California and one on Hollywood, the lucky."

"You could have had California, but you wouldn't cut in line," I said. At Gretchen's glum expression, I pushed *The Florida Story* book over to her side of the table. "Use this. Just change the name of the state."

"I can't write about Florida and make it sound like North Dakota!"

"Sure you can. Instead of alligators, just put rattlesnakes. Where it says palm trees, put sage-brush. Easy as pie."

"Honestly, Kobie," she said scathingly. "You think everybody can get away with the stuff you do."

I shrugged and flipped *The Florida Story* aside. I was making up my own Florida story, and it was probably better than the one in the library book. Gretchen did not approve. I wondered if she was a tiny bit jealous, because my report was almost done and she'd just started.

"Kobie, you can't make up *all* of your report," Gretchen said as she scanned the *World Book*. "Miss Price will give you an F."

"So what. I have to let her know I think her assignments stink. Did you hear her say we're having two music Wednesdays in a row? Because we made Halloween decorations last week? I suppose she thought that cutting out pumpkins was real art."

"I'm glad," Gretchen said. "I don't need any more creative time."

"What creative time? We haven't *had* any since the warden took over." After adding the final touches to my drawing, I looked it over, satisfied.

Actually, my Florida state report was pretty creative. My alligator picture, for instance. It had huge open jaws, ready to chomp a woman's leg. I wondered if Miss Price would notice I had drawn *her* leg, even down to the shoe she had on today.

The alligator illustrated a paragraph about the

Cypress Swamp, which came after a paragraph about the Everglades. I drew crocodiles on the Everglades page. The only good thing about Florida was that it had lots of swamps and reptiles to write about. The other stuff we were supposed to include in our reports, like climate and population and cities, was too boring for words. I didn't even feel like copying from the encyclopedia. I just made up my own facts.

Gretchen skimmed the "City" section of my report. " 'Clearwater is one place where people in Florida go in Tampa, Florida,' " she read out loud. " 'Tourists take a hotel nearby and with time off from packing they ride a glass-bottomed boat to Clearwater.' " She put the paper down and looked at me. "Where did you get this from?"

"My mother went to Florida once," I replied. "She told me about riding in a glass-bottomed boat. I'm not sure where she went, but Clearwater sounded like a good place to ride a glass-bottomed boat." It made me feel closer to my mother to write about her long-ago trip, even if I did have to fill in the gaps.

"Kobie, this part of your report is only two sentences." Gretchen pointed out.

"It's long enough," I said, already tired of this whole state report business. "Listen, stop worrying about these dumb reports. I've got more important problems."

My mother had been in the hospital so long I'd lost count of the days. I talked to her every day but I still wasn't allowed to see her. Last night she told me that her doctor said she could walk around soon. Then she'd be able to visit me in the hospital lobby. Poor Mom. She thought everything was fine at home. She didn't know she was rapidly being replaced by Mrs. Blevins. And even though I'd tried, I hadn't helped my mother's cause much.

"Gretchen, what am I going to do?" I moaned. "I've been a Holy Terror for ages, and Mrs. Blevins hasn't *mentioned* quitting!"

Gretchen turned to the *Ways Kobie Can Be Awful* list in her Nifty notebook. "You messed the house up every day?"

I nodded. "Before school *and* after. Today I emptied the garbage all over the floor before I ran for the bus. Mrs. Blevins didn't say a word."

"And you tangled up her knitting?"

"Tied it in knots!" I replied emphatically. "Plus I hid her glasses once. But Dad made me give them back to her. I can't think of anything else to *do*, except lock her out."

"You mean you haven't done that yet?" Gretchen asked, only half serious. "Kobie, I wish I could help you, but I don't have any more ideas. My brain is scrambled enough trying to write a double report."

"Will you forget about that stupid report for one second?" I demanded, annoyed. Sometimes Gretchen got on my nerves, always fretting over school.

"I can't forget it," she flared. "The report counts as half our geography grade. The state capitals test is the other half. If I don't get at least a C, my parents will take away one night of TV time."

At the beginning of the year, Gretchen's parents made a rule — any grade on her report card lower than a C would cost her a night of TV watching. The way things were in my house now, I could watch TV until the test pattern came on the air, and nobody would care. Well, Dad would. He still made me go to bed at nine, but that was probably because he wanted to watch *his* programs.

Then I wondered what would happen if I stayed up all night, flat-out refused to go to bed. Maybe Dad would see that Mrs. Blevins had no control over me, and he'd go get my mother.

"Gretchen," I said suddenly. "Have you ever stayed up all night before?"

She thought a moment. "I tried to last summer. I made a bet with Charles. Whoever fell asleep first had to make the other person's bed the rest of the summer."

"What happened?"

"I lost. According to Charles, I fell asleep right after midnight. At least that's what he *said*," she related in that special tone reserved for her big brother. Charles could be a pain sometimes. "I really tried to stay awake, but I couldn't."

"I can. I know I can. I'm going to stay awake tonight," I declared eagerly. "All night. Dad will realize that Mrs. Blevins can't do a thing with me, and he'll bring Mom back home to make me behave. And it'll be good-bye, Mrs. Blevins!"

Luck was on my side, for once. Dad had to work late again, and then he'd visit Mom at the hospital. He was going to have a late supper in the hospital cafeteria. It would be after eleven when he came home, at least two hours past my normal bedtime.

Wanting to lull Mrs. Blevins into a false sense of security, I messed up the house only a little. The rest of the evening I watched TV quietly.

At nine o'clock, Mrs. Blevins looked up from her snarled knitting, which she was patiently trying to unknot. "Kobie, dear. Isn't it time for you to change into your nightgown?"

Reaching up to switch the channel, I replied blandly, "I'm not going to bed tonight. I'm going to stay up."

"Not go to bed!" Mrs. Blevins laughed. "Oh, Kobie. You say the funniest things. You are a caution!"

"I'm not kidding," I said.

"Why, of course, you're going to bed. You need your sleep so you'll be alert in school tomorrow."

I couldn't be alert in Miss Price's class even if a three-ring circus performed in our room.

"Sleep is just a habit," I said. "I've slept at least eight hours every night since I was born. I figure I've saved up enough sleep to stay up tonight."

Mrs. Blevins smiled indulgently. "Why do you want to stay up all night?"

"So I can see what comes on TV after I go to bed." I stretched out on the floor, making myself comfortable. "I bet there's a whole other world that goes on after nine o'clock."

She stood up, abandoning her knitting. She knew she had to get me in bed before my father came home. If he found me up, he'd be furious. Probably fire her on the spot.

Mrs. Blevins tried her level best to make me sleepy so I'd go to bed. First she brought a pillow and quilt.

"Put this under your head," she said, handing me the pillow. Then she tucked the quilt around me. "It's chilly on the floor. I wouldn't want you to catch cold."

The soft pillow and warm quilt made me feel very cozy. I probably would have fallen asleep right there in front of the TV, but the program was exciting, with a lot of murders and yelling.

When she saw the blanket and pillow trick didn't work, Mrs. Blevins fixed me a mug of hot milk. Everybody knows hot milk makes a person drowsy. She couldn't fool me *that* easily.

I rolled out of my quilt nest. "I'd rather have a Coke. And some barbequed Fritos."

"Kobie, it's almost ten-thirty," Mrs. Blevins said. "Fizzy drinks will keep you up all night."

"That's the idea." I got up to get my snack. I was munching on Fritos when Dad came home.

"Hello, everybody," he said. Then he realized how late it was. "Kobie, why are you still up? It's way past your bedtime."

Mrs. Blevins laughed. "Kobie's playing a game."

"No, I'm not," I said. Mrs. Blevins didn't look very worried, but I knew she was probably sweating it out. Her job was on the line.

Dad playfully swatted my backside with his cap. "Okay, Kobie, off to bed. No more foolishness."

"I want to stay up all night," I said in a convincing tone. "It won't hurt me, Dad. I'm not the least bit sleepy. I probably couldn't go to sleep even if I went to bed. I'd just toss and turn all night."

He sighed. "Kobie, why must you be so difficult? You know the rules. Bedtime is nine o'clock."

"Yes, but it's already after eleven and nothing bad has happened to me — "

"Not yet," he said ominously.

"Dad, rules don't make sense sometimes. Why should I go to bed just because the clock says a certain time?" He was weakening, I could tell. It was hard to argue with sound logic.

"Let me stay up just this once," I wheedled. "If I get sleepy, I promise I'll go right to bed. Cross my heart and hope to die, stick a needle in my eye." I made the necessary motions to seal my promise.

"All right, all right," Dad relented at last. "You can stay up. But if I come out here and find you asleep on the floor, I'll ground you this weekend. That means no TV, no going out, no phone."

"I won't fall asleep," I said brightly. "I'm wide awake as a bat." I blinked to prove my wide-awakeness.

"Well, *I'm* going to bed," Mrs. Blevins declared. "Do you need anything else tonight, Mr. Roberts?"

"No, thanks."

"I do," I piped up. "I could use another Coke, this time with extra ice, and — "

"Kobie," Dad scolded. "Don't push your luck. Good night."

"See you in the morning." I switched the channel to a better station.

"Turn that off," he ordered. "Even if you don't want to sleep, other people have to get their rest."

"I can't watch television?" I cried, horrified. Watching TV all night was the whole *purpose* of staying up. That and getting Mrs. Blevins fired. "Can I watch it if I leave the sound off?"

My father agreed to television with no sound and one light on. While he and Mrs. Blevins were getting ready for bed, I rushed into my room to get some things.

I brought out all my stuffed animals and lined them up on the floor against the sofa, so I would have plenty of company. I also brought out drawing paper, crayons, pencils, a deck of cards, and my new library book, *Pippi in the South Seas*. This was going to be such fun!

I'd be just like Pippi Longstocking, who stayed up all night and went to bed when she wanted. Life for Pippi was one long party.

In the darkened kitchen, I refilled my Coke glass and emptied crumbs from the Frito bag into a bowl. Not much of a midnight snack, but better than nothing.

Then I hopped back into the living room and settled down in front of the TV. Mrs. Blevins had lost, I told myself smugly. Dad probably didn't want to chew her out in front of me, but I knew he'd fire her first thing in the morning. My mother's job was saved!

Happily I planned my all-nighter. I could draw for two hours and then read for an hour and draw another two hours and then play cards for an hour. . . . It was like having a whole extra day, free to do as I pleased.

Taking a fresh sheet of paper, I started drawing. The light from the flickering TV and the single lamp I was allowed to have on cast shadows across my paper. It was tough to draw in such poor light. After a while, I gave it up.

Rearranging the quilt and pillow, I lay back to watch television. Without any sound, I couldn't really tell what was going on. Too bad I never learned to read lips. The silent, leaping images on the screen made my head hurt, so I stopped watching. I left the TV on, though, because I was feeling a little lonely. And very alone.

The house was so quiet . . . and *dark*. The small lamp didn't provide much light, not when there was so much darkness to hold off. I edged closer and closer to the lamp, trying not to think about things I shouldn't think about at night. Like that there was somebody sneaking up the basement steps, slowly, one step at a time. Any second, the doorknob would turn —

I grabbed the deck of cards like a life preserver. A rousing game of solitaire would banish scary thoughts. The only problem was, I didn't know *how* to play solitaire. I'd seen other people play the game, which seemed to consist of laying down rows of cards and frowning a lot.

I plunked down nine cards in a row, face down. Then I plunked nine cards on top of those, face up. I frowned a lot, mainly because I had no idea what I was doing. Also, because I was afraid.

Where was the guy coming up the basement steps? Up to the top step yet?

The late show went off and a news program came on. The announcer's mouth flew open and shut like a mousetrap as he described horrible silent news stories, the kind they couldn't tell on regular news programs. He was probably warning everybody in Willow Springs about a prowler right this minute. . . .

I turned the television off. The square of light, my only contact with the human race, collapsed inward until it was just a dot. I flicked the set back on.

One-thirty. How long until morning? When *was* dawn, officially? Four o'clock? I tried to count the hours until then, but I kept yawning. My eyelids wanted to clank shut, but I propped them open with my fingers. That woke me up a little.

I tried to read my Pippi Longstocking book, but the print was like ants crawling across the pages. I couldn't draw, I couldn't read or watch TV. What a drag. Was this what grown-ups did when they stayed up all night?

A noise made me snap to attention. Was that a creaking floorboard? Had the prowler climbed the stairs and was now sneaking around the house, cloaked in shadow? My heart lurched into my throat. I should go wake my father, but I couldn't move. It was like a bad dream — I felt rooted to the spot.

In the hall, a white shape wavered uncertainly.

I clamped my hand over my mouth, fighting a scream. It wasn't a prowler, but a ghost!

"Kobie," the ghost whispered, approaching on furry feet. "Are you okay?"

The ghost was only Mrs. Blevins, wearing a white nightgown and fuzzy slippers.

"You scared me," I said hoarsely.

"You're very sleepy," she whispered. "Let me help you to bed."

"I don't want to go to bed." My words were slurred.

Mrs. Blevins helped me to my feet. "I know. It's hard to give up when you've fought this long." She steered me gently to my room.

I fell across my bed like a sack of cement. Someone untied my tennis shoes and slipped them off. I felt the covers being pulled up around my shoulders.

I'd lost again, but I was too worn out to do anything about it. I hoped my mother would understand.

# 11

On the morning of the state capitals test, I was in a rotten mood. Not because I hadn't studied for the test. I *hadn't* studied, but I wasn't worried about my dumb geography grade the way Gretchen was.

Being a Holy Terror, I'd discovered, was hard work. I had been awful going on three weeks now and Mrs. Blevins still thought I was Little Miss Mary Sunshine. The woman was impossible.

Today I wore my skirt inside-out and my shirt on backwards, plus a pair of my father's work socks. When she saw my outlandish attire, Mrs. Blevins merely smiled. My mother would never have let me go to school dressed like that, but Mrs. Blevins thought I was "very original," as she put it.

"Aren't you tired of wearing weird clothes?" Gretchen asked, staring at the seams of my inside-out skirt.

"Believe it or not, I am. But I don't know what else to do, Gretch. I'd wear my head on backwards if I could get rid of Mrs. Blevins."

Nosy Lynette O'Bannon turned around in her seat. "It's bad luck to wear your clothes backwards. You'll have bad luck all day."

"It's bad luck to sit behind you," I retorted. Lynette and her stupid superstitions! If she hadn't made me mad enough to step on every crack that time just to spite her, my mother wouldn't be in the hospital with a bad back.

"Clear your desks, except for one sharpened pencil," Miss Price announced.

I handed Gretchen my pencil. "Will you sharpen mine for me? My legs won't make it up to the pencil sharpener."

"What's the matter with your legs?" Gretchen asked. "You're walking funny."

"You'd walk funny too if you lived under a card table." My latest scheme to drive Mrs. Blevins away sounded really good when I originally dreamed it up.

Two days ago, I set the card table up in the middle of the living room floor and draped a sheet over it, like a tent. I told Mrs. Blevins that the card table was my new house and I wasn't coming out for anything except to use the bathroom and go to bed. (Staying up all night made me appreciate my bed more than ever.)

I moved my books, crayons, and smallest stuffed animals (because there wasn't much room) into my new house. Mrs. Blevins cheerfully delivered my meals to the card table, lifting up the sheet to pass me the tray. When I was through, I pushed the tray through the sheet, sort of like room service.

At first it wasn't so bad living under a card table. I pretended I was camping out. But it was pretty cramped and I couldn't do anything except read or draw pictures. I couldn't even watch television. When I crawled out to go to bed, I could hardly walk. My legs felt crippled from being bent like pretzels all those hours under the table.

"If Mrs. Blevins doesn't leave soon so my mother can come home, *I'm* going to need traction," I remarked.

Gretchen went up to sharpen our pencils. Putting mine in the little trough on my desk, she said, "Kobie, Thanksgiving isn't that far away. Won't your mother be home by then anyway?"

"That's what she keeps telling me on the phone," I replied skeptically. "Mom doesn't know the truth, that Mrs. Blevins has just about replaced her." I shook my head to emphasize the seriousness of the situation. "My mother is never coming home."

Gretchen's eyes were round with sympathy. "Oh, Kobie. Your poor mother."

"Poor me, you mean! If my mother doesn't come home, I'll have to spend the rest of my life under a card table."

Miss Price gave a bunch of dittos to the first

person in the row to pass back. "If you studied, you should do well on this test," she said. "The answers are right on the test sheet. All you have to do is match the state with its capital. You will have fifteen minutes."

Lynette tossed my test sheet over her shoulder. It missed my desktop and landed on the floor.

"Pick it up," I said. "You're supposed to hand it to me, not throw it."

Busy answering the test questions, Lynette ignored me.

In a louder voice, I said, "If you don't pick it up, I'm telling the teacher. Besides, you started before Miss Price said we could."

"Kobie," Miss Price said. "What's the problem back there?"

"Lynette threw my test sheet at me." I managed to sound very injured. "I guess she's in a hurry to begin the test."

"No one is to begin until I give the signal. That includes you, Lynette. Give Kobie her test sheet."

Lynette bent down and slapped my test sheet on my desk so hard I was surprised she didn't leave a hand-shaped dent on the desktop. "Tattletale," she whispered angrily.

"Now you know how it feels," I hissed back.

"Stop it, you guys," Gretchen whispered worriedly. "We're all going to get in trouble."

Miss Price waited until everyone had sheets, then said, "Ready? You may begin."

The test was ridiculous, just like I knew it would be. The states were in alphabetical order down the left margin, followed by a blank space. Jumbled-up capitals filled the column on the right.

I wrote down the few capitals I knew. Honolulu for Hawaii. Richmond for Virginia. Some of the names were a dead give-away, like Indianapolis for Indiana. I tried to make that work for Annapolis, but there wasn't a state called Annapolia.

Beside me, Gretchen nervously chewed her bottom lip as she scribbled capital after capital. She had to get a C so she wouldn't lose a day of TV. I thought about copying her paper, but I didn't want to get her in trouble. If Miss Price caught a kid cheating, she tore up the cheater's paper and the person's paper he was copying from. Miss Price had some crummy rules. Why punish both kids?

To pass the time, I matched capitals with any old state, thinking I might get a few of them right just by chance. Then I turned my paper over so Miss Price would know I was done.

Gretchen was still working. So was Lynette. I could see the bottom half of Lynette's paper if I looked over her shoulder. She had just written, "Augutsa" in the space beside Maine, instead of "Augusta." The teacher marked down for misspelling. If Lynette was any kind of a friend, I would have kicked her desk or something to let her know she had made a mistake. But Lynette probably wouldn't have appreciated the favor.

Bored, I glanced around the room. Nobody else had finished yet. I glimpsed a drawing sticking out of Lynette's cubbyhole, a picture of her dog. It was pretty good, I grudgingly admitted to myself. Lynette was a tattletale teacher's pet, but she was also a good artist. Too bad I couldn't stand her.

I scooted up to get a better look at the drawing. Lynette had used the side of her pencil to shade the dog's fur. I couldn't draw fur or hair very well yet. Maybe I should try Lynette's technique to make fur look more realistic. I inched forward a little more, wondering if she had used short or long strokes.

"Kobie Roberts!" Miss Price's sharp voice startled me. "To the front of the room, please. Lynette, I want to see you, too. Right now, girls. And bring your test papers."

"Me?" Lynette pointed to herself in astonishment. "What did I do?"

"Just come to the front. No arguing." Miss Price looked furious.

I hustled up to Miss Price's desk with my test paper. Lynette was right behind me. We handed our papers to Miss Price. She ripped them in half and dropped the halves in the trash can beside her desk.

Lynette's mouth formed an O. She was stunned. So was I.

"What'd we do?" I demanded.

"Kobie, I saw you looking at Lynette's paper. You know what happens to cheaters," Miss Price replied.

Lynette's face crumpled. She was going to cry, the sissy baby. She got on my nerves something awful, but she didn't deserve to fail the test. Neither of us had done anything wrong.

"I didn't cheat," I said stoutly. "I was already finished. My paper was turned over."

"I saw you looking over Lynette's shoulder," Miss Price insisted.

"I was looking at a drawing sticking out of her desk," I explained. "I wasn't cheating. Look at my paper. I probably got them all wrong because I didn't study."

"Well, *I* did," Lynette wailed. "I studied hard and you made me get a zero! I hate you, Kobie Roberts!"

As much as I disliked Lynette O'Bannon, I didn't want to her to flunk the test because of me. It really wasn't her fault. It wasn't *my* fault, either, but I couldn't make Miss Price believe me.

"Why don't you ask Gretchen to come up here?" I suggested. "She'll tell you I had my paper face down when I was looking at Lynette's drawing."

Miss Price hesitated, then she crooked her finger at Gretchen, who was watching the whole scene with big eyes.

Gretchen was a shaky witness. I figured she was thinking that her paper would be ripped in half, too, just for being involved. I hated putting my best friend on the spot, but I knew Gretchen would tell the truth. I hoped Miss Price realized that Gretchen never lied.

"Kobie claims she was already finished and her paper was face down on her desk. Is that true, Gretchen?" Miss Price grilled.

Gretchen swallowed hard and nodded. "I saw Kobie turn her paper over. She was finished before anybody. Then she scooted up a little bit to look at this picture sticking out of Lynette's desk. That's all she was doing, Miss Price. Honest."

Miss Price still didn't seem convinced. Lynette kept bawling. Gretchen looked as if *she* might cry. The three of us were going to get zeros unless I did something quick.

I fished the test papers out of the trash can and put the two halves together. "Just look at my paper," I said to Miss Price. "Compare it to Lynette's. My answers are different from hers. If I were cheating, then wouldn't my answers be the same as hers?" I pointed at a line on the test paper. "See? Lynette put 'Augutsa' for Maine. I have 'Boise.' I didn't study a lick. My answers are all wrong."

Now Miss Price directed her stern expression solely at me. "Why didn't you study, Kobie? You knew this test was coming up." Her tone was different. I could tell she finally believed me.

The others were off the hook, I felt certain, so

I could say exactly what I thought without risking their grades.

"I didn't study because I think the test is dumb," I said bluntly. "We do the same things Mr. Breg's class does. Nobody likes Mr. Breg," I added dangerously.

"And so nobody likes me, either?" Miss Price concluded, her eyebrows arched.

"I do," Lynette said heartily. Naturally, the teacher's pet would jump in to score a few Brownie points.

Miss Price Scotch-taped our test papers back together. "You may go back to your seats," she told Lynette and Gretchen. "Kobie, wait here."

From the center drawer, she took out a letter she had already written, scribbled a sentence at the bottom, then put it in an envelope and sealed it. "Take these to Mrs. Victor," she said, handing me the envelope and my taped-together test paper, along with a hall pass.

As soon as I was near a window, I pressed the envelope to the glass, hoping to read what was inside. Unfortunately, the paper was too thick.

Mrs. Victor was sitting at Mr. Leon's old desk. She seemed happy to see me. Then she opened the envelope and read the letter.

"Kobie, Kobie, Kobie," she sighed. "What are we going to do with you? Miss Price says you deliberately failed the state capitals test. Because, as she says *you* said, it was dumb."

"It *is* dumb. I mean, who cares about the capital of North Dakota? I'm never going there."

"You might, one day," Mrs. Victor allowed. "But even if you don't, you should know something about the world around you. Even more important, you should try to get *along* in the world. You make everything so hard, Kobie."

"No, I don't," I argued. "It's Miss Price. *She's* the one who makes everything hard. I loved fifth grade until she came." I decided to change the subject to a safer topic, away from myself. "Are you going to be the principal for the whole year?" I inquired innocently.

"Not the whole year — " she began.

I nearly jumped with joy. "Mr. Leon is coming back?" If the principal could come back to school, then my mother was sure to come back home!

Mrs. Victor shook her head. "No, Kobie, he isn't. Mr. Leon is better, but he decided to retire early. We're getting a new principal in the spring. April or May. I'll be his assistant, to help him get used to his new job."

My heart sank. Mrs. Victor was never coming back to Room 8. My mother wasn't coming back home. That meant I was stuck with the substitute teacher and the housekeeper forever.

"In the meantime, you must try to get along with Miss Price," Mrs. Victor advised. "She likes you, Kobie. She really does. But you don't make it easy for her."

"She doesn't make it easy for me, either."

Mrs. Victor jotted a few sentences at the bottom of Miss Price's note. Then she slid it into the envelope. She didn't seal it, though.

"You may go back to class," she said, giving me the envelope. "Think about what I said."

I flew out of the office. Gretchen was dawdling over a long drink at the water fountain. She had the other hall pass tucked under the arm.

"Kobie!" she cried. "I've been waiting for you."

I clutched Gretchen's arm. "What is it? Did Miss Price tear up your test anyway? I'm sorry I asked her to call on you, but it was the only thing I could think of. She was going to give Lynette a zero and it wasn't fair."

"You mean you actually saved Lynette's grade? I thought you couldn't stand her."

"I can't, but I still don't want her to flunk because of me. Everything's okay?"

Gretchen nodded. "Everything is okay with us, but I've been worried about you. What happened with Mrs. Victor?"

"Nothing. Mrs. Victor talked to me. She wrote on Miss Price's note. I'm going to read it." I slipped the letter from its envelope.

"Kobie, you can't read that!" Gretchen gasped, shocked. "You're always eavesdropping and spying on people."

"It's the only way I find out stuff," I said. "Anyway, this isn't eavesdropping. More like eaves-peeping."

"But it's a federal offense. You could go to jail."

Too late. I couldn't stop reading if Mrs. Victor herself caught me.

"Miss Price says that I need a challenge!" I reported in amazement. "She says I'm clearly bored with school work, and I need a project of my own! Can you *believe* it?"

"What else does she say?" Gretchen asked, suddenly curious.

"She asked Mrs. Victor if it would be all right to let me do the fairy tale theater."

I had forgotten all about the fairy tale theater. So Miss Price was going to go ahead with the project after all. And I was going to be one of the artists!

At the bottom of the letter, Mrs. Victor had added in her neat handwriting, *Give Kobie another challenge. Let Lynette O'Bannon be the second artist on the project. She and Kobie have a lot in common.*

"What does she mean by that?" I said.

"Maybe she means you're both good artists," Gretchen guessed. "Or maybe she means you two ought to be friends."

I shook my head. "I still don't know how working with Lynette would be a challenge. No way do I have a thing in common with her. Absolutely no way."

# 12

"I'll draw the scenes with the mice and horses and stuff," I told Lynette as we stretched the long roll of light brown paper across the floor. "Because I draw animals good. You draw the scenes with Cinderella in her ball gown because you like to draw fancy dresses."

Lynette sat back on her heels. "You know what would be neat? If we put glitter on Cinderella's ball gown. That would make it sparkle like real jewels."

I opened the Golden Book of *Cinderella* we were going to copy from, noticing that Cinderella's blue dress *did* sparkle. "That's a great idea. I'll buy the glitter."

"I have a brand-new box of crayons. We can share," she offered, smoothing a wrinkle in the paper. She looked at me and smiled. "This is going to be fun, isn't it?"

After Miss Price announced who the theater artists were, Lynette and I haggled one entire day over what fairy tale we would illustrate. She wanted to do *Sleeping Beauty*, but I thought *Cinderella* was more exciting. And there were more animals in that story. Finally Lynette agreed with me.

Miss Price bought us the Golden Book so Lynette and I could decide which scenes we would use in our story scroll. I couldn't believe how well we were getting along. We both wanted to make this the best theater story Room 8 had ever done.

Lynette and I were allowed to work on the scroll a half hour in the morning and a half hour right after lunch. I could tell the other kids in our class were a little bit jealous because we got out of doing regular work an hour a day.

Lynette wasn't such a goody-goody when we were working together, I discovered. She had neat ideas, and she didn't talk about school stuff when we were drawing. Karen Heinz didn't like Lynette spending so much time with me so she started hanging around Susan Riley.

Gretchen came over. "Which picture are you going to do first?" she asked, paging through the book.

"You do the title and the credits," I said to Lynette. "And I'll do the first scene."

Lynette wasn't born yesterday. "Uh-uh, Kobie. We both work on every single scene, together."

"But if we split the scenes, it'll go faster," I said.

"I guess you don't need me," Gretchen said,

almost to herself. She went back to her seat and got out the list of spelling words for the week.

"Lynette — " I began, still trying to convince her I was right.

Just then Miss Price signaled us to return to our seats.

"We've completed our unit on geography," Miss Price said as she handed back our graded reports. "Tomorrow we begin social studies. I enjoyed your state reports very much. They were all very interesting."

"If she liked those dumb reports, she probably reads the phone book for fun," I muttered to Gretchen.

Gretchen didn't look at me. She was probably anxious about her geography grade.

Lynette received her report first. "I got an A!"

"You had a cinchy state," I said. "Hollywood and movie stars."

Then I received my report. "I don't even want to see my grade." I tossed my Florida report on Gretchen's desk. "You look for me."

She opened the cover. "Kobie, you got an A minus!"

"What?" I couldn't believe it. "I made the whole thing up! How could she give me an A?"

"Miss Price only marked two words you misspelled," Gretchen said.

I burst out laughing. "She must like creative writing!"

"She likes you." Gretchen's voice was small and wistful.

"Me? You must be joking," I snorted. "Here's your report. Gretch. You aced an A plus, easy."

Gretchen opened the cover of her report, then shut it quickly. "I got a C plus," she whispered, mortified.

"C plus!" I bellowed. "That's totally unfair! You worked harder than *any*body on your report."

"There weren't any books on North and South Dakota," Gretchen said miserably. "I didn't write much. . . . She marked me down because of it."

"I told you you should have made it up — " I began, but Gretchen slammed her fist down on her desk.

"I don't make up reports! And I don't cut in line! I don't do the things you do, Kobie Roberts. I can't be like you." Her face was a shade I'd never seen before, a dark, mottled red.

I was flabbergasted. Gretchen wasn't mad at Miss Price for giving her a crummy grade — she was mad at *me!* Then I realized that Gretchen was almost in tears.

"Listen," I said. "If it'll make you feel any better, I'll go tell Miss Price I made up my Florida report. Maybe she gave us the wrong grades. That's it! I should have gotten the C and you should have gotten my A minus. It's just a mix-up, Gretch."

"It's not a mix-up!" she denied miserably. "It's

147

the way things *are*. Teachers always like your work, Kobie, because you're creative. They like creative kids."

I wasn't so sure about that. According to Miss Price, I created disturbances more than anything.

"No, they don't," I disagreed. "Remember what Miss Price did to my Halloween decoration."

"Some sixth-grader put your decoration over the trash cans. Miss Price loves your drawing. See the pictures hanging on the bulletin board? They're all yours and Lynette's. But mostly yours. Have I ever had a drawing on the bulletin board?" she asked. We both knew the painful answer. "I'm just a dull stick — all I can do is memorize capitals and copy stuff from encyclopedias. No wonder I got a C."

In all our years of friendship, I never realized Gretchen felt bad because my drawings were on the bulletin board and hers weren't. She always said she didn't like creative time, especially art, and I thought it was because she'd rather do spelling or something. Miss Price should have been thrilled to have a kid like Gretchen in her class — Gretchen was the perfect student. She was good without being a goody-goody like Lynette. Everybody got along with her.

But I suppose that being good made her feel invisible, something I'd never be in a million years. Maybe Gretchen actually *wanted* to be creative, so she'd be noticed. Gretchen was truly special — a lot more special than I'd ever be. And yet I got the A minus and the theater project. If only Miss Price had picked Gretchen instead of Lynette to be the second artist on the theater scroll.

I considered asking Miss Price to take Lynette off the project, but I knew Lynette would pitch a fit and besides, her feelings would be hurt. Lynette was sort of becoming a friend.

Then I decided Miss Price ought to take *me* off the project. Put Gretchen in my place. But I couldn't give up the theater project. Gretchen probably wouldn't like drawing mice and pumpkin coaches.

"Time for music," Miss Price said, getting the instruments from the closet.

Music Wednesday. The day was going from bad to worse. With a huge sigh, I stuffed my Florida report in the cubby under my desk. Gretchen put hers away quietly and sat with her hands folded. I knew she was still trying to keep from crying.

Today our song was "Michael, Row Your Boat Ashore." First Miss Price handed out the idiot instruments, the blocks and spoons and triangles. Gretchen got a pair of blocks. Lynette got a set of spoons. I didn't get anything, which suited me just fine.

Then Miss Price gave out the real instruments. Vincent Wheatly lucked out and got the xylophone. And miracle of miracles, Miss Price ac-

149

tually handed *me* the tambourine! I nearly swooned.

I tapped the tambourine against my palm, making the silvery disks jingle. The kids with the blocks and spoons and triangles looked enviously at my tambourine. I tapped it again.

Then I noticed Gretchen sitting as stiffly as the wooden blocks on her desk. She didn't congratulate me for finally landing a decent instrument. I wondered if she was thinking that Miss Price picked me to play the tambourine because I was so creative.

It struck me that Miss Price was just being nice, giving me the theater project and the tambourine in the same week. She really seemed to be on my side. On second glance, I decided her lips weren't mean at all. I should try to be nicer to her. And to my best friend, while I was at it.

"Are we ready?" Miss Price said when all the instruments had been distributed.

I raised my hand. "I don't want the tambourine."

She stared at me. "You don't want the tambourine? Kobie, are you going to be difficult again — "

"No, really," I said in my sweetest voice. "You know, Miss Price, I have no musical talent." I thumped the tambourine like it was a garbage can lid. "I've decided I'd rather play the blocks. I'll just trade with Gretchen."

Reaching over, I swept the blocks off Gretchen's desk and plunked the tambourine in her lap. Gretchen's eyes widened. Gingerly she picked up the tambourine and gave it a tentative jangle. Then she grinned at me.

Miss Price was smiling, too. "I think you made a very good decision, Kobie Roberts."

I did, too. In fact, making my best friend happy was probably one of the best decisions I'd made all year. Making peace with my new teacher wasn't such a bad idea, either.

The class orchestra began to saw away at "Michael, Row Your Boat Ashore." Gretchen played the tambourine pretty well. She hit it against the heel of her hand on the right notes, as I smacked my blocks together. Attempting to make music with two wooden blocks was still impossible, but I didn't mind. For the first time, I actually enjoyed music Wednesday.

Gretchen and I were best friends. I had a new project to work on, and maybe another friend. My teacher appeared to be on my side. Everything was almost perfect, except I was still half an orphan.

If only my mother would come home. . . .

Mrs. Blevins told me about my father as soon as I walked in the door.

"He called to say he would be late again. Some trouble at Burke Elementary."

Probably another dumb kid had pitched the manhole cover down the sewer. At least it wouldn't take Dad long to crawl down the ladder and locate the missing manhole cover. He shouldn't be too late tonight.

"Will he stop and see Mom?" I asked Mrs. Blevins.

"He didn't know for sure," she replied, heading into the kitchen to start supper. She seemed a little distracted. Usually she asked me how my day went, what I learned in school, and so forth. Maybe she was finally tired of living in the same house with a Holy Terror.

Which reminded me I had an act to keep up. In my room, I changed from my school skirt and sweater to my best Sunday dress.

"I'm going up on the hill," I said to Mrs. Blevins.

She eyed my outfit. "You're not going to dig in that good dress?"

"Yes, I am," I said defiantly. My mother only let me wear the pink dress on very special occasions. She'd throw a net over me before she'd let me run outdoors in that dress, much less hike in the woods. But Mrs. Blevins merely nodded.

It was warm for November. I didn't even need a jacket. The wind was blowing pretty briskly, though. Leaves skipped across the yard to collect in a swirling pile against the side of the house.

Up on the hill, it was even windier. I hadn't been up here in several days. My roller coaster track didn't look like a track at all, but an aimless little line scratched in the dirt. I don't know why I ever thought I could make a carnival ride with a pick and a broken-down scooter. It was a dumb idea.

Dejected, I slouched on the log. Ever since my mother went to the hospital, my life was like that roller coaster track. A scrawny crooked line going nowhere. I thought I would like being on my own, staying up all night, eating what I wanted. But those things weren't any fun, I found.

I scraped at a loose piece of bark. The air seemed strange, kind of purplish, as if a neighbor were burning leaves. The woods were very quiet. I knew most of the birds had already gone south for the winter, but usually there was a sparrow hopping around in the brush or a squirrel scurrying to bury acorns. The more I sat there, the more I realized something was wrong.

Maybe it was my mother. Maybe something awful had happened to her!

With my heart in my throat, I ran down the hill, snagging my best dress on blackberry vines. I burst into the kitchen and demanded, "Did my mother call yet?"

Mrs. Blevins turned from the stove. "No, dear. She hasn't. But she will. Don't worry. Your mother always calls."

"I'm going to call her," I said.

My mother's roommate answered the phone.

My mother was taking physical therapy, in another part of the hospital. The roommate, an older woman, reassured me that my mother was fine and that she'd call me back later.

But I couldn't shake the nagging sense that something was wrong.

We ate supper, just the two of us. When we finished, I ducked under the card table set up in the living room and tried to read my library book. Mrs. Blevins clicked the radio on for company while she did the dishes.

Radio Report Card came on the air, so I knew it was seven-thirty. Kids could call the station if they had a question about their homework, and a teacher would answer it for them. One time I heard Vincent Wheatly call in and ask what was one plus one in this fake baby voice. He pretended he couldn't understand the answer and made the radio-teacher explain it over and over.

My book was good, but I couldn't concentrate on Pippi's exciting adventures. If only Mom would call me back, so I'd know for certain she was okay.

On the radio, a boy asked what the square root of twenty-seven was. The teacher began a lengthy reply but was suddenly interrupted. The news announcer cut in with a special report.

"We've just received word that Burke Elementary School, in the Fairfax City area of Fairfax, is on fire," the announcer said. "The blaze started after school had been dismissed, although we don't

154

have details on the cause of the fire. Three area fire and rescue companies are on the scene. We'll bring you an update on this and other news on WEAM Newswatch, on the hour."

I flew out from under the card table, dragging the sheet with me.

"Dad's at that school!" I cried to Mrs. Blevins, who came hurrying from the kitchen with soapy hands. "Dad's in that fire!"

"He didn't tell me the school was on fire," she said excitedly. "Maybe it wasn't much of a fire when he heard about it. Three fire companies! It must be a terrible fire."

"Dad's going to be killed!" I screamed.

Mrs. Blevins put her arms around me. "No, he isn't, lamb. He'll be just fine. Your father doesn't work for the fire department, remember? He works for the school board. He's probably waiting for the firemen to put out the fire so he and his men can clean up. A fire makes a dreadful mess, you know."

Sobs clogged my throat. I couldn't speak. Now I knew what terrible thing was happening. It wasn't my mother who was in danger, but my *father*.

Before the night was over, I would no longer be half an orphan. I'd be a whole orphan.

# 13

Mrs. Blevins knew exactly what to do. She moved the radio by the telephone and pulled up two chairs, so we could hear both. Then she sat me in the most comfortable of the chairs and brought me Ellsworth, my favorite stuffed animal.

"Mom is going to call back," I said, willing a tear that had filled my right eye not to fall. I didn't want to cry in front of the housekeeper. "What am I going to say to her? She doesn't know about Dad."

"If you want, I'll talk to her," Mrs. Blevins offered. "But we really don't know anything, Kobie. We ought not to worry your poor mother, in the hospital and all."

As it turned out, when my mother did call me back, she was drowsy from the whirlpool bath she had just taken. Mom asked me what I had done in school that day, and I told her about working on the "Cinderella" project with Lynette. She kept yawning and finally she said she was too sleepy to make sense. She said good-night and hung up.

"She doesn't know about the fire," I said to Mrs. Blevins. "She knows Dad's working late because he didn't visit her at the hospital."

"You spared your mother a lot of worry," Mrs. Blevins said approvingly. "And that wasn't easy to do. You're a good girl, Kobie. I'm sure your parents are very proud of you."

The first tear, the one I'd been trying to hold back, slid down my nose. It was quickly followed by another.

"I'm not a good girl," I whimpered. "I used to be, according to my mother, but I'm not anymore."

"Of course you are, lamb." Mrs. Blevins patted my knee.

"No, I'm not," I contradicted, crying in earnest now. "It's my fault my mother is in the hospital." I told her about the day Lynette dared me to step on a crack and how, in sheer defiance, I boldly stepped on all the cracks. "And now Dad's at this terrible fire. I probably did something to put him in danger, too."

Mrs. Blevins turned my shoulders, forcing me to look at her. "Kobie, you are not responsible for your mother's back condition."

"But I stepped on all those cracks!"

"That's an old superstition. You're much too bright to believe in such nonsense, I know you

157

are." Her tone was firm but kind, as always. "You haven't done anything to hurt your parents. Get that notion out of your head, right this minute."

It was easy for her to talk. I doubted she had ever done a mean thing or thought a mean thought in her entire life. I wasn't even ten and a half yet, and already I had a record a mile long.

Gretchen would probably grow up to be like Mrs. Blevins, the kind of person kids adored. And me? I'd probably grow up to be like Mrs. Settinger, the grouchy cafeteria lady, the kind of person little kids had nightmares about.

As if she could read my mind, Mrs. Blevins began telling me about something she had done a long time ago.

"When I was nine," she said in a soothing bedtime-story voice, "I had a falling-out with my mother. It was summer, I remember, and I decided to run away from home."

I curled up in my chair. I liked stories about the olden days.

Mrs. Blevins' blue eyes grew far-away with recollection. "We lived in the Knolls' place then, just outside of Manassas. It wasn't the Knolls' house, of course. It was ours, and this happened before we sold the house to Mr. Knolls. Anyway, we lived in that big old two-story house. It was early in the summer — we hadn't put the screens on the windows yet. Well, anyway, my mother sent me to my room after our argument. I rolled up a bundle of clothes and opened my window and threw the clothes bundle out first. I was going to climb down the old rose trellis."

I tried to picture dumpling-shaped Mrs. Blevins clambering down a rickety rose trellis.

Mrs. Blevins started chuckling. "I threw the clothes on my mother's head!" she exclaimed. "My mother was right beneath my window, working on her roses! The clothes hit her on the head, wham! She didn't say anything, and I didn't notice she was down there. I backed out of the window and started to climb down. When I got close to the bottom, this voice said, 'Going somewhere, Ada?' "

"Is that your name?" I asked.

She nodded. "When I saw Mama standing there, holding my clothes, I nearly jumped clear back up to the second-floor window. She scared me that much. Instead I jumped the rest of the way and lit out across the yard, running to beat the band. Mama ran after me. We ran all over that yard, and through the garden and through the woods behind the garden. Mama was right behind me the whole way. I never knew she could run that fast!"

"My mother can run, too," I put in, remembering a few of our backyard chases. "Then what happened?"

Mrs. Blevins laughed. "We both ran out of steam. We walked back to the house, gasping for breath. My mother wore cotton stockings and they were ripped to shreds. I'll never forget that, my mother's stocking hanging in strings. She sent me back up to my room to continue my punishment, and no more was said about our little race through the woods."

"You didn't try to run away again?"

"Nope. I learned my lesson. You can't run away from your mother, no matter how fast your legs go!"

I considered her last statement. "I didn't try to run away from my parents. I drove them away," I said morosely.

"Oh, Kobie," Mrs. Blevins sighed. "You want to grow up in a hurry. You act like you don't need anybody. But we know that isn't true, is it?"

"No." I did need my parents. And my teacher. And my friends.

"It's hard getting along in this world all by yourself," Mrs. Blevins added gently.

I started crying again. She was right. "What am I going to do?" I sobbed. "My parents are gone!"

"They'll be back. The worst will be over tonight, Kobie. You mark my words."

At nine o'clock the radio news stated that the fire was burning out of control. At nine-thirty, the news announcer reported that the fire was finally under control, but that Burke Elementary was a total loss.

"Where will those poor children go to school?" Mrs. Blevins wondered aloud as she brought us hot chocolate and big slices of pound cake.

If I hadn't been so worried about my father, I would have gladly traded places with any of those "poor children" who attended Burke Elementary. Having your school burn to the ground is every kid's fondest dream.

At ten-fifteen, the phone rang. I was dozing in the chair, so Mrs. Blevins answered it. I was awake in an instant, but she was already hanging up the receiver.

"It was your father," she told me. "He's all right. He couldn't talk to you because a lot of men were waiting to call their wives, and he still had to call your mother."

"Is he coming home?"

"Not yet. The fire is out, and now they have to clean up. Make sure they get rid of smoldering furniture and things. He won't be home until tomorrow morning, Kobie. You might as well go to bed. Everything is all right."

Everything *wasn't* all right and wouldn't be until both of my parents were home safe, but I went to bed anyway. I was worn out from worrying.

Mrs. Blevins tucked me in. "When you wake up, your father will be here to kiss his little lamb good morning."

"Will you be here, too?" I asked sleepily.

She seemed surprised by the question. "Of course I'll be here, Kobie. I'm staying as long as you need me."

As she bent over to pull the blanket up to my chin, I caught a whiff of her rose cologne and thought about a young Mrs. Blevins climbing down a rose trellis after she had bonked her mother on the head with her clothes bundle. Mrs. Blevins was a real person, not just someone who cooked and cleaned. I liked her a lot.

"Would you kiss me good-night?" I whispered shyly.

Mrs. Blevins kissed me on both cheeks, very softly. "Good-night, Kobie, dear," she said, leaving the door open a crack so the light from the hallway fell across the foot of my bed.

A bumpity noise woke me. I sat up, my mind crowded with the events of the night before. The sky was beginning to turn from gray to pink. It was morning, but just barely.

Sliding out of bed, I shrugged into my bathrobe and ran out of my room. The living room and kitchen lights were blazing merrily. The mingling aromas of coffee and bacon teased my nose. Mrs. Blevins was up, too.

The side door opened and my father came in, carrying a huge box which he set heavily on the living room floor beside another huge carton. That explained the bumpity noise.

"Dad!" I cried, launching myself at him.

"Kobie," he laughed. "What are you doing up at this hour? Don't get too close, I'm positively filthy."

"I don't care," I said, even though he *was* dirty and smelled like charcoal.

Mrs. Blevins came in from the kitchen, drying her hands on a tea towel. "Kobie, go put your slippers on. The floor is cold."

Dad unwound my arms from around his neck. "Listen to Mrs. Blevins, Kobie. And then I'll show you what I brought you."

"Those boxes are for me?" I said incredulously. Breaking the world speed record, I dashed into my room for my slippers and ran back to the living room.

Dad was sitting on a kitchen chair Mrs. Blevins brought in so he wouldn't get the upholstered furniture dirty. His face was streaked with soot and his hands were like a coal miner's. He looked exhausted, as if he might fall asleep sitting up.

"These are all mine?" I asked again, tearing the flaps of the biggest box. "What's in them?"

"Booty from the fire," Dad replied, sipping the coffee Mrs. Blevins just handed him.

I reached deep into the box, even though the strong acrid smell of smoke drifted up from the contents, and brought out a handful of . . . paper! The box was completely filled with paper! Loose-leaf paper, packets of construction paper, tablets

163

of that wide-lined paper the primary grades used, colored paper, unlined paper, more paper than I had ever seen in my life. The edges curled upward, singed brown, but aside from that, the paper was perfectly good. And it was all mine! My greatest wish, next to having my mother home, had come true.

"You can cut off the brown part," Dad said.

"How did you get all this paper?" I asked. "I thought the school burned to the ground."

"The building is still there. The inside is a total loss, though. Everything is going to be thrown away, even the desks. As the firemen cleared each section, my men and I went in to bring out any combustibles — anything that might catch fire again." He indicated the boxes. "Early in the evening, I cleaned out the supply room, so this stuff isn't too badly damaged. I brought you the best of the lot."

Eagerly, I tore into the next box. This one contained supplies of all sorts, pens, pencils, pencil boxes, erasers, compasses, rulers, boxes of colored chalk. Crayons were melted into a colorless waxy lump. I laughed as I held up the crayon blob.

Dad grinned. "I guess the heat was too much for them."

"That's okay. Lynette has a new box of crayons she's letting me use at school." I kept pulling wonderful supplies out of the carton. I could set up my own school store, I had so much stuff. There

164

was a slim, pointed pen that wrote turquoise ink I particularly loved. And a stencil ruler that had the letters of the alphabet cut into it.

At the bottom was a flat object. I leaned way inside to pull it out. It was a Nifty notebook, just like Gretchen's!

I balanced the notebook on my knees and regarded it wonderingly. Then I lifted the magnetic flap and revealed the secret compartments. I placed the turquoise pen in the narrow compartment.

"Dad," I said. "This is just so great. Thanks so much. I don't know how you had time to remember me, fighting a fire and all."

"How could I forget my little artist at home? Like I said, the paper and supplies were just going to be thrown away. There's a school desk out on the porch, too."

A desk! What other surprises did he have for me?

Mrs. Blevins called him in to breakfast. "Let your father eat, Kobie. He's been up all night and needs to go to bed."

I helped Dad walk into the kitchen where an enormous breakfast of French toast and bacon and eggs was waiting.

"What, no pancakes and gravy?" he joked. We all laughed.

"One more thing," Dad said before he began eating. "I talked to your mother just after I left the school. She didn't get much sleep, either, I'm afraid. Her doctor came in late last night and told her she could walk around now. I'll take you with me to the hospital this evening."

I was going to see my mother! "I want to wear my good pink dress," I told Mrs. Blevins. "And I have to make Mom a card. Right this minute." I scampered back to the boxes of supplies to select what I'd need.

"Before school?" Mrs. Blevins wanted to know. "Before daylight?"

"Yes!" I called back, rooting through the box of paper to find just the right sheet for my mother's card.

The hospital lobby was a big disappointment. There weren't any sick people or any blood and guts. Just a bunch of potted rubber plants and beige sofas. There was one guy in a wheelchair talking to a woman, probably his wife. I eyed him closely to see if he had anything visibly wrong with him, but then Dad told me all the patients went around in wheelchairs, even though most of them could walk.

At last the nurse brought Mom downstairs. She grinned from her wheelchair when she saw me. I ran to her, clutching the card I had made her.

"Mom! Your back looks so straight. Can I hug you?"

She reached out for me. "Sure you can hug me.

I won't snap in two. Oh, Kobie, I can't believe how you've grown. That dress is too short. Turn around."

I modeled the pink dress, which Mrs. Blevins had mended so Mom wouldn't detect the rips from when I wore the dress in the woods.

"I bet you've gained five pounds," she declared. "Mrs. Blevins must be feeding you well."

"She's a good cook," I said, then added hastily, "but not as good as you. When are you coming home?"

"Next week," she said, smiling.

I handed her the construction paper envelope. "Open your card."

The drawing in the front showed me whizzing down a roller coaster dip. I was alone in the roller coaster car. Underneath the picture I had written, "Life is no joy ride without you." On the inside I wrote in big letters, "Hurry home. Your one and only daughter."

My mother's eyes misted over, and she dabbed at them with the corner of her bathrobe. "Why, Kobie, I think you really missed me."

I sat down on the floor so I could put my head in her lap. "Yes," I said, my voice muffled in her bathrobe. "I'm tired of being on my own. It's a lot of work."

She and Dad laughed. My mother stroked my hair. I had forgotten how good it felt to have her do that.

"I thought you didn't need anybody," she said. "Didn't you tell me that once? That you didn't even need a friend."

"I do need a friend," I said. "Maybe even two friends. And I need my teacher, even if she doesn't know much about art."

"What about your parents?" Mom prompted.

"Especially my parents." Double for my mother.

Mom hooked my hair behind my ear. "Well, you'll be on your own soon enough, Kobie. When you're ready, it won't be so hard. You'll enjoy it. But remember to stop by and visit your aging parents, will you?"

I wondered when I would be ready to be on my own entirely. Maybe when I was eleven. Or maybe when I was a little older.

I wasn't *quite* ready to leave home yet. There were a million projects I hadn't even thought of, much less done, and a whole boxful of paper to use.

What more could a kid ask for?

# About the Author

CANDICE F. RANSOM lives in Centreville, Virginia, with her husband and black cat. She writes books for young people and enjoys going out to eat whenever she can.

Her popular Kobie books are based on her own experiences growing up. Ms. Ransom says, "My brain stops at about age fifteen. I'm a grown-up by default." Some of her books include, *My Sister, the Meanie*; *My Sister, the Traitor*; *My Sister, the Creep*; and *Millicent the Magnificent*.